# THE
# TRAILSMAN
#374

# FORT
# DEATH

## by

## Jon Sharpe

A SIGNET BOOK

SIGNET
Published by New American Library, a division of
Penguin Group (USA) Inc., 375 Hudson Street,
New York, New York 10014, USA
Penguin Group (Canada), 90 Eglinton Avenue East, Suite 700, Toronto,
Ontario M4P 2Y3, Canada (a division of Pearson Penguin Canada Inc.)
Penguin Books Ltd., 80 Strand, London WC2R 0RL, England
Penguin Ireland, 25 St. Stephen's Green, Dublin 2,
Ireland (a division of Penguin Books Ltd.)
Penguin Group (Australia), 250 Camberwell Road, Camberwell, Victoria 3124,
Australia (a division of Pearson Australia Group Pty. Ltd.)
Penguin Books India Pvt. Ltd., 11 Community Centre, Panchsheel Park,
New Delhi - 110 017, India
Penguin Group (NZ), 67 Apollo Drive, Rosedale, Auckland 0632,
New Zealand (a division of Pearson New Zealand Ltd.)
Penguin Books (South Africa) (Pty.) Ltd., 24 Sturdee Avenue,
Rosebank, Johannesburg 2196, South Africa

Penguin Books Ltd., Registered Offices:
80 Strand, London WC2R 0RL, England

First published by Signet, an imprint of New American Library,
a division of Penguin Group (USA) Inc.

First Printing, December 2012
10  9  8  7  6  5  4  3  2  1

The first chapter of this book previously appeared in *Utah Terror*, the three
hundred seventy-third volume in this series.

Copyright © Penguin Group (USA) Inc., 2012

 REGISTERED TRADEMARK—MARCA REGISTRADA

Printed in the United States of America

PUBLISHER'S NOTE
This is a work of fiction. Names, characters, places, and incidents either are the
product of the author's imagination or are used fictitiously, and any resemblance to
actual persons, living or dead, business establishments, events, or locales is entirely
coincidental.

The publisher does not have any control over and does not assume any re-
sponsibility for author or third-party Web sites or their content.

ALWAYS LEARNING                                                    PEARSON

# The Trailsman

Beginnings . . . they bend the tree and they mark the man. Skye Fargo was born when he was eighteen. Terror was his midwife, vengeance his first cry. Killing spawned Skye Fargo, ruthless, cold-blooded murder. Out of the acrid smoke of gunpowder still hanging in the air, he rose, cried out a promise never forgotten.

The Trailsman they began to call him all across the West: searcher, scout, hunter, the man who could see where others only looked, his skills for hire but not his soul, the man who lived each day to the fullest, yet trailed each tomorrow. Skye Fargo, the Trailsman, the seeker who could take the wildness of a land and the wanting of a woman and make them his own.

*1861, in the heart of hostile country—someone
is killing scouts, and they have the
Trailsman in their gun sights.*

# 1

The shot came out of nowhere.

One moment Skye Fargo was riding along a winding track in the Salt River Range, and the next a lead hornet buzzed his ear even as the boom of a rifle shattered the morning air.

Fargo reacted instinctively. With a jab of his spurs, he reined the Ovaro behind a slab of rock and dismounted. Yanking his Henry rifle from the saddle scabbard, he moved to where he could see the slope he thought the shot came from.

A big man, broad of shoulder and narrow at the hips, Fargo wore clothes typical of his profession: buckskins, boots, and a high-crowned hat. A Colt that had seen a lot of use was strapped around his waist, and a red bandanna in need of washing was around his neck.

Fargo's lake blue eyes narrowed. He scanned the pines and spruce and firs without spotting the bushwhacker. He'd heard reports the Bannocks were acting up of late, so it could be a hostile.

Or it could be an outlaw. He was far from any settlement, farther from any town or city, deep in the haunts of those who preyed on the unwary.

Either he waited the bastard out, or he went after him.

Fargo hunkered, the Henry across his legs. He had plenty of patience, and he wasn't due at Fort Carlson for another three days.

The post was named after the commanding officer. It had been built specifically to keep the Bannocks and a few other tribes in check. Instead, it had stirred them up.

Time crawled.

Fargo refused to show himself until he was sure it was safe. And he wasn't thinking of just his hide. Anyone who knew prime horseflesh would love to get their hands on his stallion.

He took pride in the Ovaro. It was as fine a mount as any. If the shooter had brought it down, he wouldn't rest until the bastard was worm food.

Half an hour went by. Fargo was about convinced the culprit was gone when a shadow moved among the pines. Instantly, he snapped the Henry to his shoulder, fixed a bead, and fired.

There was no outcry. It could be he'd fired at a deer or some other animal, but he doubted it.

Sinking onto his belly, Fargo crawled around the boulder and over to a log. Removing his hat, he raised his head high enough to see. Almost instantly a rifle cracked and slivers stung his cheek and brow.

Fargo ducked low. He touched his cheek and a drop of blood formed on his fingertip. He'd been lucky a second time—that shot damn near took out his eye.

Jamming his hat back on, Fargo crawled around the log and into high brush. When he had snaked about ten yards he eased up into a crouch.

The woods were silent. The birds had stopped chirping and warbling, the squirrels had ceased their chatter.

Again Fargo wondered if it might be Bannocks. The latest word was that a band of young hotheads was killing every white they came across.

Above him, something moved. Someone was slinking down the slope in his direction, using every bit of cover to be had.

"Got you," Fargo said under his breath, and grimly smiled. Whoever ambushed him was about to learn that he wasn't the forgive-and-forget type. He was more an eye-for-an-eye hombre, and the devil be damned.

Fargo centered the Henry's sights on a two-legged shape but it promptly disappeared. Whoever it was, they were skilled at woodcraft.

Fargo did more waiting. All he wanted was a clear shot.

The sun climbed and no one appeared.

Fargo didn't like it. The shooter should be near enough by now for him to see or hear. He was about to rise and commence a hunt when he heard a sound that spiked him with rare fear: the Ovaro nickered.

Throwing caution to the wind, Fargo heaved erect and raced back. The shooter had circled and gone for his horse. Should the Bannocks get their hands on it, he'd likely never see it again.

He was so concerned for the Ovaro, he barreled around the rock slab with no thought to his own hide—and dug in his boot heels as a rifle muzzle blossomed practically in front of his face.

He had no time to level the Henry or draw his Colt.

He was as good as dead.

The rifle was a Sharps, and the man holding it had more whiskers than Moses. The man grinned and said, "Bang. You're dead."

For one of the few times in his life, Fargo was flabbergasted.

"What's the matter, pup?" the bearded man taunted. "Cat got your tongue?" At that he lowered the Sharps and let out a hearty laugh that more resembled the rumble of a bear.

"You son of a bitch," Fargo said, and hit him.

The punch rocked the other man onto his heels. Where most would have been mad and resorted to their hardware, the bearded bushwhacker only laughed harder. "You should have seen the look on your puss," he whooped, and roared anew with giant mirth.

A flood of emotions washed through Fargo: anger, resentment, relief, and finally amusement. Despite himself, he indulged in a good laugh of his own. "You're the craziest bastard I ever met, Tom. That stunt could have got you killed."

Bear River Tom, as he was known, was twice Fargo's age, with a craggy face and ruddy cheeks and a nose a moose would envy. He wore buckskins, except the whangs on his were a foot and a half long and swished with every movement of his bulky body. "I got you, pup!" he crowed with glee. "I had you spooked. Admit it."

"You could have blown my head off, you jackass."

"If that was my intent, your brains would be leaking out of your noggin right this minute," Bear River Tom boasted. "You know how good a shot I am."

Yes, Fargo did, but that didn't excuse the practical joke. He reminded himself that Tom had always been the rowdiest scout on the frontier. "What if I'd shot you before I knew who it was?"

"That would have been plumb embarrassing."

Fargo shook his head, and sighed. "What are you doing in this neck of the woods, anyhow?"

"I got me an invite," Bear River Tom said. "From a pard of ours."

"You too?" Fargo said, thinking of the short letter he'd received from California Jim, a fellow member of the scouting fraternity. He slipped his fingers into a pocket and touched it. "I got mine pretty near a month ago."

"Same here," Bear River Tom said. "Wonder why he wants to see us."

Fargo shrugged. He reckoned that California Jim had a good reason. They'd been friends a long spell.

"It'll be great to see him again," Bear River Tom said. Placing the stock of his Sharps on the ground, he leaned on the barrel. "So tell me, pup. Ever been to the Salt River Range before?"

"Been through it several times."

"Know it like the back of your hand, then?"

"Not that well," Fargo admitted. He'd always been on his way somewhere else. "What difference does it make?"

Bear River Tom shrugged. "Just asking. I don't know this country well, either." He gazed out over the array of peaks and verdant forest. "Fort Carlson wasn't built that long ago. The only scout I heard of working out of it is Badger."

"Emmett Badger?"

"Ain't he enough?" Bear River Tom said, and chuckled. "That coon has more bark on him than all these trees put together."

Fargo grunted in agreement. Emmett Badger had a reputation for being one of the toughest scouts alive. That took some doing, given that scouts were generally a hardy bunch who could hold their own with the Sioux and the Apaches.

"How about we fetch my cayuse and we'll ride on to the fort together?" Bear River Tom proposed.

Fargo grunted again. "Why not?" He wouldn't mind the company. Shoving the Henry into the saddle scabbard, he forked leather.

Bear River Tom was eyeing the Ovaro as if the stallion were a saloon filly. "That's a damn fine animal you've got there. You ever get in a mind to part with it, let me know."

"Part with?" Fargo said, and patted the Ovaro's neck. "Not while I'm breathing."

"Didn't think so. Word is that if it was a mare, you'd marry it."

"Go to hell."

Laughing, Bear River Tom cradled his Sharps and led the way up the mountain. As they passed through ranks of blue spruce he breathed deep and remarked, "God Almighty, I love the wilds. The mountains, the prairies, the deserts."

"Makes two of us," Fargo said.

"The only thing I love more than the wilds," Bear River Tom said, "are tits."

"Don't start," Fargo said.

"Yes, sir," Bear River Tom said. "I love a handful of tit more than just about anything."

"Here we go again," Fargo said.

"Fact is, when you think about it, tits should turn as many folks to religion as the Bible does."

"Were you in the outhouse when they were passing out brains?"

5

"Hear me out. Who else but the Almighty could have made it so tits are so much a part of our life from the cradle to the grave."

"I've lost your trail," Fargo told him.

"Think about it. We suck on tits for the milk when we're infants, we suck on tits when we're older to poke the females who have the infants who suck on the same tits for the milk, and we dream about tits in our old age to help pass the time. If that doesn't show planning, I don't know what does. God must like tits as much as we do." Bear River Tom grinned at his own brilliance. "You can see I'm right, can't you?"

"I need a drink," Fargo said.

# 2

When most people back in the East thought of a fort, they imagined high wooden palisades. They also imagined wide gates and ramparts and cramped living space for the officers and enlisted men.

That wasn't always the case west of the Mississippi.

Fort Carlson, for instance. It had no palisades, no walls of any kind. The buildings were spread out in a horseshoe smack in the middle of the Salt River Valley. Starting at one end, there was the blacksmith's, the sutler's, the guard-house, company headquarters, a few homes for the senior officers, long barracks for everyone else, plus a stable and an attached corral.

"God Almighty, will you look at that," Bear River Tom marveled.

Fargo was looking. All the buildings and sheds and out-houses had been painted white. Even the corral posts and rails. "I'm surprised they didn't paint the parade ground white, too."

Bear River Tom laughed. "I heard the commander had it done to give the place a civilized look."

"No wonder Indians think whites are touched in the head."

"We are," Bear River Tom said. "Heads in a whirl is how the Shoshones would put it."

"You lived with them a while, didn't you?"

"For half a year or so. I took up with a Shoshone gal. Her people are right friendly. They adopted me into the tribe. I wasn't the first white they did that with. There's a mountain man they adopted years ago. I met him and his spooky son once."

"Spooky?"

"The son is a man-killer."

"Who isn't these days?"

They gigged their horses and wound along the Salt River, the surface gleaming bright in the sunlight. Butterflies flitted about the wildflowers that grew along the banks.

"I reckon killing is a way of life out here, sure enough," Bear River Tom continued their conversation. "What with red killing white and white killing red and white killing white and red killing red, there's plenty of killing going around. It's sort of like catching a cold. Once you catch the killing bug, you pass it on to everybody else."

"You say the strangest damn things."

Bear River Tom chortled. "So I've been told. It probably comes from spending so much time inside my own noggin."

"There you go again."

Men in uniform and others were moving about the post. Infantry drilled on the parade ground, and a dozen cavalry were putting their mounts through their paces.

"Look at 'em," Bear River Tom said. "It's a regular beehive."

Sentries were posted fifty yards out, and a soldier with the V's of a corporal on his sleeves moved to intercept them. "Hold up," the trooper said, shifting his rifle and raising a hand. "Halt and be recognized."

Bear River Tom snorted and drew rein. "You can't tell we're white?"

"As dark as you two are," the corporal said, "either of you could about pass for redskins. You're scouts, by the look of you."

"And you halt us anyway?"

"Orders are orders," the corporal said, and looked them up and down. "Now we have more of your kind than we can shake a stick at."

"Emmett Badger is still here then?" Bear River Tom said.

"He's the official scout. Colonel Carlson swears by him." The corporal paused. "I was talking about the others."

"Others?" Fargo asked.

"Four, besides you two and Badger," the corporal clarified. "What's going on, anyhow? How come so many scouts are showing up at one time?"

"Beats the hell out of me," Bear River Tom said.

"Is one of the four California Jim?" Fargo wanted to learn.

"There's a gent by that name, yes," the corporal said. "Old cuss. He calls me a whippersnapper, and me pushing thirty."

"That sounds like Jim."

The corporal motioned. "Well, go on in, seeing as how you're white and all."

"We're obliged, general," Bear River Tom said.

"You're not funny," the corporal said.

"Depends on whose mirror you're looking into," Bear River Tom rejoined.

"Huh?" the man said.

New arrivals were a rarity. Fargo wasn't surprised that nearly everyone gave them a close scrutiny. They rode to a hitch rail in front of the company headquarters, and dismounted.

Arching his back, Fargo stretched. He'd ridden for over a week to get there. It would be nice to rest up for a couple of days.

The lieutenant drilling the infantry was barking commands in sharp cadence. Farther out, the cavalry paced their horses in unison.

"Got to hand it to the boys in blue," Bear River Tom said. "They sure work hard."

A voice behind them said, "I'm happy to hear you think so highly of us."

They turned.

A man with a colonel's insignia had stepped from the

headquarters. Ramrod-straight, his uniform spotless, he stood with his hands clasped behind his back as if he were at parade rest.

"You must be Carlson," Bear River Tom said.

"*Colonel* Carlson," the commanding officer corrected him.

"Must make you proud," Bear River Tom said. "It's not every day a man has a post named after him."

"The army didn't know what else to call it," Colonel Carlson said. "And it won't be here forever. As soon as the Bannocks are suppressed, the army will close it down and move us elsewhere."

"Suppressed?" Bear River Tom said. "Is that a fancy word for on a reservation or killed off?"

"Whatever it takes," Colonel Carlson said. "The red menace must be contained."

Fargo bristled. He had a hunch the colonel was one of those who believed the only good Indian was a dead Indian. "The Indians were here before we were."

Colonel Carlson regarded him icily. "I suppose you're one of those who has lived with them."

"I have."

"And mated with them."

"That's one way of putting it."

"So have I," Bear River Tom broke in. "And a nice mating it was." He chuckled. "Tits are tits, I always say."

The colonel switched his icy stare to him. "Did you just say *tits*?"

"They're his favorite thing," Fargo said.

Bear River Tom nodded enthusiastically. "Every man I know likes tits. And it beats saying bunions all hollow."

"Bunions?" Colonel Carlson said.

"Can't fondle them, now can you?"

Colonel Carlson sniffed. "Scouts." He said the word as if it were a plague. "You are all alike."

"We love tits," Bear River Tom said.

"That's enough," Colonel Carlson said. "There are women on this post, and I won't have them overhear your vulgarity."

"You have something against t—" Bear River Tom caught himself. "Against melons?"

"I'm not as obsessed with them as you obviously are," Colonel Carlson informed him.

"Maybe you should be," Bear River Tom said. "There's nothing that helps a man relax like a handful of jugs."

Colonel Carlson closed his eyes and raised his hand to his nose and pinched the bridge as if he had a headache, or was about to. "Why are you gentlemen here? I don't recall sending for more of your ilk, yet I find myself in scouts up to my neck."

"Ilk?" Bear River Tom said. "I'm fit as a fiddle."

Fargo snorted.

"Emmett Badger is my scout," Colonel Carlson said. "I don't need any others. Yet now six more have shown up. And I imagine you'll give me the same story they did. That you were sent for by one of your own."

"That I was," Bear River Tom said. "By Badger himself."

"What?" Fargo said.

"We talked about his letter earlier," Bear River Tom said.

"My letter is from California Jim."

"What?"

Colonel Carlson's brow knit. "Interesting. You'll find it even more so when you talk to the rest."

"In what way?" Bear River Tom asked.

"It's common knowledge that scouts enjoy playing practical jokes," the commanding officer said. "But the purpose to this one eludes me."

"What joke?" Fargo asked.

Colonel Carlson smiled. "You'll find out directly." He smoothed his uniform and started past them but stopped. "A word of caution. It's also common knowledge that scouts enjoy raising hell. There will be none of that here. I run my post strictly by the book. Any shenanigans and there will be consequences. Do I make myself clear?"

"Hell no," Bear River Tom said. "Can't you use little words like everybody else?"

"Mock me if you must," Colonel Carlson said. "Although I should think you would want to stay in my good graces." He nodded at each of them and strolled toward the parade ground.

"He sure is fond of himself," Bear River Tom said. "And has a broom up his ass, to boot."

Fargo was more interested in something else. "What did he mean by a practical joke?"

"Let's find out."

They made for the sutler's. Along the way they had to pass the guardhouse, and when Fargo glanced over, he saw a face peering out at them. It stopped him in his tracks. "What the hell?"

"What is it, pup?"

Fargo bobbed his chin at the swarthy visage behind the bars in a small window in the door.

"It must be one of the bucks who went on the warpath," Bear River Tom said.

They went over. A soldier was on guard but he made no attempt to stop them.

To judge by the Bannock's gray hair and wrinkles, Fargo guessed that he'd seen sixty winters or better.

His arms were folded across his chest, and he had an air of dignity about him.

"What have we here?" Bear River Tom said. "Who are you, old hoss?"

To their surprise, the old Indian cleared his throat and said, "Me Lone Bear of the Panati. You whites call us Salt River Bannocks."

"What did you do that the army took you into custody?" Fargo asked.

"Colonel Carlson come to our village. Him say me must go with him. Him say that he take me to teach my people lesson. Him say our young warriors must stop killing whites or he will do bad thing to me."

"What bad thing?" Bear River Tom asked.

"Him say he will hang me by a rope from tree until me be dead."

"Hell," Fargo said.

# 3

"Something on your mind?" Colonel Carlson asked without looking around as Fargo came up. He was watching his men drill.

"What do you think you're doing?" Fargo demanded, stepping around in front of him.

Carlson colored. "Be careful how you address me. I don't care for your tone."

"Lone Bear," Fargo said.

"What about him? He's the chief of the band that's been giving us trouble."

"The younger warriors are on the warpath. Not Lone Bear."

"He's their chief. Therefore, he's responsible. Just as I'm responsible for the behavior of the soldiers under me."

"It's not the same," Bear River Tom interjected. "A chief doesn't have the power you do. He can't order a warrior to do or not do something. He can ask, but the warriors don't have to listen."

"Then why bother being chief?" Colonel Carlson said. "And be that as it may, my strategy worked." He puffed out his chest. "Those bucks of his haven't killed a single soul since I took him into custody."

"Does Washington know?"

"I have full authority to deal with the renegades as I deem fit," Colonel Carlson informed them. "Seventeen lives have been lost because of them, and I'll be damned if anyone else will die. Anyone white, that is."

"Seventeen?" Fargo said in genuine shock.

"You didn't know that, did you?" Colonel Carlson said smugly. "That's the tally so far. Nine were members of a wagon train bound for Oregon Country. A war party struck as they were hitching their teams to their wagons." Carlson scowled. "Three of those nine were women."

Fargo scowled.

"Do you still blame me for hauling Lone Bear in?" Colonel Carlson asked. When neither of them answered right away, he said, "No? I didn't think so. I stand by my decision. So long as we hold their precious leader, the Bannocks won't lift a finger against us."

"It might turn the Bannocks who are still friendly to whites against us," Fargo felt compelled to mention.

"You don't seem to be listening. Their feelings aren't the issue here. Saving lives is." Carlson started to walk away. "Now if you'll excuse me. Some of us have work to do."

"I reckon he put us in our place, pup," Bear River Tom said.

"Come on," Fargo growled.

A few off-duty troopers were the only customers at the sutler's.

Out of curiosity Fargo went down the aisles. The selection didn't rival a general store but for the middle of nowhere there was a lot.

"May I help you?" a spindly man in a white apron asked.

"We're looking for friends of ours," Bear River Tom said. "Scouts, like us."

"I don't keep track of the post personnel," the sutler said. "But I do believe those you seek rode off with Emmett Badger along about daybreak."

"Where to?" Fargo asked.

"I'm sure I don't know," the sutler replied. "Are you positive I can't sell you anything?"

"Later maybe," Fargo said.

"It's just as well. I have stocking to do. A patrol came in yesterday and reported a wagon train will arrive in a week or so."

"Get a lot of them, do you?" Bear River Tom inquired.

"Enough to keep me in business," the sutler said. "If I relied on the soldiers for my livelihood, I'd starve."

"The army isn't lavish with its pay," Bear River Tom said.

"No, the army is not. Even if it were, Colonel Carlson keeps a tight rein on things. I can't sell liquor. Or playing cards. Or dice."

"The hell you say," Bear River Tom said.

The sutler nodded. "The liquor I can understand. But to deprive grown men of their right to indulge in friendly wagers now and then is taking discipline too far. Not that I would ever say that to the colonel's face."

"You can always close up and go elsewhere," Fargo said.

"Carlson is strict, yes, but I can live with that," the sutler said. He glanced at the entrance and bustled off.

"Nervous little fella," Bear River Tom said. "Do you know what he needs to relax?"

"Don't say it," Fargo said.

"Tits, tits, and more tits."

They went back out and leaned against the front wall and watched the drills.

After a while Bear River Tom said, "I just had me a thought. A wagon train means females. Could be they'll stick around a few days and we can get acquainted."

"Is that all you ever think of?"

"Listen to you. The randiest rooster this side of any-where," Bear River Tom said. "If you were a horse you could open your own stud farm and be in clover the rest of your days."

"Which am I? A rooster or a horse?"

"You're a bull elk in rut."

At that moment two women came strolling along the periphery of the parade ground. Both wore bonnets and long dresses that clung to their winsome legs.

"How do you do," Bear River Tom said, and licked his lips. "What have we here?"

"Officers' wives," Fargo deduced. "And off-limits unless you hanker to be beaten to a pulp by a dozen soldiers."

"Off-limits for you maybe, pup," Bear River Tom said. "For me a tit is a tit."

"I never thought I would say this," Fargo said, "but I am commencing to hate that word."

Women were not all that plentiful on the frontier, especially at military posts, and double-especially at remote posts like Fort Carlson.

"Ladies," Bear River Tom said as the pair approached, doffing his hat. "Nice day if it don't rain."

The women smiled politely and strolled inside.

Bear River Tom nudged Fargo. "Did you see that? One of them likes me."

"You're imagining things."

"The one with the brown hair. She jiggled her tits at me."

Fargo stared.

"What?" Bear River Tom said. "I saw them jiggle with my own eyes."

"Were you hit on the head when you were a sprout? Or did a tree fall on you sometime?"

"I tell you she did. I am a master at tits. And some females jiggle theirs to get a man's attention."

"She has a dress on."

"So?"

"And under that, likely a chemise."

"So?"

"And under that maybe more."

"You're saying that even if she did jiggle her jugs, I couldn't see them for all her clothes."

Fargo grinned. "I'll be damned. There's a smidgen of smart left in that head of yours."

"You have to have real good eyes to catch a tit jiggle," Bear River Tom said. "You should get yours checked. Might be you need spectacles."

"Might be I need a drink more than ever," Fargo said.

He turned, debating where to go next, and spied a rider

in buckskins trotting toward the post from across the valley. "Look there."

"A scout, by-God," Bear River Tom said.

"We can't be sure from this far off," Fargo said. A lot of people besides scouts wore buckskins—backwoodsmen, trappers, some farmers and the like.

"It's those bad eyes of yours," Bear River Tom said. "If you can't see tits at three feet, how can you expect to tell who is who from that far away?"

Fargo hoped it wasn't a scout just to prove Tom wrong. But as luck would have it, he wasn't.

"It's California Jim!"

Fargo smiled. Of all the scouts, he liked California the most. Jim's nickname came from the fact he was always going on about how when he finally got too old to scout, he would head for California to spend his remaining days lying in the sun and listening to the surf roll in. Jim was as fond of oceans as Bear River Tom was of tits. Well, almost.

"I wonder where the others are."

Fargo moved out from under the overhang, took off his hat, and waved it.

California Jim straightened, waved his own hat, and brought his horse to a gallop. With a whoop and a holler, he pounded up in a swirl of dust and was out of the saddle before his animal stopped moving. "Skye, you ornery coon!" His buckskins were decorated with blue and red beads, and he wore a blue bandanna that hung near to his waist. He wore a black gun belt decorated with silver conchos, and a high-crowned hat that was popular in Texas. Clapping Fargo on the shoulders, he declared, "You're a sight for sore eyes!"

"How have you been?" Fargo asked.

"My joints creak more." California beamed. "God, it's good to see you again."

"Kiss him, why don't you?" Bear River Tom said.

California ignored him and clapped Fargo again.

"Haven't seen you since that time in the Mountains of No Return. We were lucky to get out of there alive."

"What am I, chopped liver?" Bear River Tom asked.

California Jim finally looked at him. "What you are is a tit fiend and a damned nuisance."

Fargo laughed.

"I'm a tit what?" Bear River Tom said.

"You heard me. I'm warning you now. Go on about tits like you usually do and I will by-God take my rifle stock to your head."

"That's harsh," Tom said.

California Jim turned back to Fargo. "You won't believe it, but the last time I ran into him, we had drinks in a saloon, and damn me if he didn't talk about tits for four solid hours."

"I believe it," Fargo said.

"A man can never have enough tits," Bear River Tom said.

"What brought you here, hoss?" California Jim asked Fargo. "I bet it was a letter."

"From you, in fact," Fargo said.

California swore. "Which I never sent. I'm here because I got a letter from you."

"The hell you say," Fargo said.

"All of us scouts got letters, which none of us sent," California Jim said, and scratched his stubble. "What in tarnation is going on, pard?"

Fargo wished he knew.

# 4

To say the scouts were puzzled was putting it mildly. As California explained, the scouts who had already arrived decided to get away from the fort to hash things over. So earlier that morning they'd saddled up and ridden into the mountains to the east of the valley. They'd climbed a short way to a clearing, and three of them were seated around a fire drinking coffee when Fargo and his friends came out of the trees.

Emmett Badger was the first on his feet. A small man, he had a reputation for being as hard as iron. His buckskins were plain, and he favored Apache-style knee-high moccasins instead of boots. He was the only scout Fargo knew who never wore a hat. Instead, Badger let his mane of dark hair fall past his shoulders. His face was bronzed, his eyes twin flints. He didn't smile or greet them; he simply nodded.

The other two scouts Fargo had never met before.

Jed Crow knew the Rockies as good as anyone. Crow wasn't his real name. He'd been born Jedidiah Mortimer Flavenbush in New York City, of all places. He'd come west and ended up taking a Crow gal for a wife. When her people adopted him, he adopted their name as his own to show how honored he was.

The last scout, Tennessee, was named after the state he was from. He never gave his real handle. Lanky to the point of being skin and bones, Tennessee wore green buckskins and a coonskin cap. He favored an old Kentucky rifle that had been in his family for generations.

Fargo and Bear River Tom shook hands with each of them and joined them at the fire.

"Ain't this something," California Jim declared. "The cream of the scouts, all in one place at one time."

"There are supposed to be seven of us," Fargo remembered the sentry and the colonel saying. "Who isn't here?"

"That would be me," said a voice in the woods, and the next moment a buckskin-clad form sashayed into the clearing.

"I'll be damned," Bear River Tom said. "A scout with tits."

"Gentlemen," California Jim said, "I don't believe either of you have made the lady's acquaintance. This here is Sagebrush Sadie."

Fargo had heard of her. Everyone had. The only female scout on the frontier. The sole survivor of the Beckwirth Massacre, Sadie had been taken in by a kindly couple down to Fort Laramie. They'd tried to teach her ladylike ways, or so the story went, but she'd taken to shooting and riding and doing all the things men could do, only better. And somehow or other she became a bona fide scout.

Gossip had it she was a looker. But the gossip got it only half right. She was stunning. Even clad in buckskins and wearing boots and a hat with a curled brim and a feather, she was one of the prettiest females Fargo ever set eyes on.

Her face was oval, with high cheekbones and full red lips and eyes as green as emeralds. Her buckskins fit her so tight, they might as well be her skin. Her full breasts and the shapely curve to her thighs were enough to bring a lump to any man's throat. On top of all that, she moved with an unconscious sway of her hips that set Fargo to stirring below his belt.

"Heard of you, gal," Bear River Tom said, rising and introducing himself. "And goodness, aren't you a sight?"

His eyes were fixed on her chest.

Sagebrush Sadie had a Spencer rifle in her left hand and a Remington revolver on her left hip. In addition, the hilt of a bowie jutted from the top of her left boot. Smiling, she walked up to Tom and he extended his huge hand to shake. Still smiling, Sadie suddenly jammed the Spencer's muzzle into his groin.

"What the hell?"

"Keep staring at me like that," Sadie said sweetly, "and I will put one in your pecker."

Bear River Tom looked down. "Here now. I don't look at you any different than I do any other woman."

"I've heard about you," Sagebrush Sadie said. "About how fond you are of these." To Fargo's amazement, she cupped one of her breasts, her fingers splayed wide.

"Good Gawd," Tennessee blurted in a thick Southern accent.

Bear River Tom's Adam's apple bobbed. "I think I'm in love."

The *click* of the Spencer's hammer froze all of them.

"I reckon I'm not making myself clear," Sadie said. "I won't be treated like a saloon tramp. I won't be ogled, by you or any other man. The next time you look at me that way, there'll be hell to pay."

"A fella can't help it when a gal is as good-looking as you."

Sagebrush Sadie's smile widened. "You better help it, you horny bastard, or you'll be carrying your balls around in a pickle jar."

California Jim cackled.

Sadie stepped back and cradled her Spencer and came around the fire. She stopped in front of Fargo and raked him from hat to spurs. "You have to be the famous Skye Fargo."

"I do?"

"As many times as I've heard you described," Sadie said. "Handsome as hell, they say. And for once they got it right."

"Here we go," California Jim said.

"Hush, old man," Sadie said. "Do you ride every horse you admire?"

"What?" California Jim said in confusion. "Why no, of course I don't."

"Neither do I." Sadie hadn't taken her sparkling green eyes off of Fargo. "So don't you 'Here we go' me, you hear?"

Several of the scouts grinned, but not Emmett Badger.

"Enough of this foolishness," he growled. "We didn't come up here to talk about your love life. Make cow eyes at him some other time."

Sagebrush Sadie faced around. "Are you telling me what to do?"

"Uh-oh," Tennessee said.

Badger's hard features became harder. "You don't want to rile me."

"Oh, don't I?" Sagebrush Sadie said archly, placing her free hand on her hip. "In case you ain't heard, no one tells me how to behave. Not ever."

Badger wasn't intimidated in the least. "*I'm* telling you to quit your flirting so we can hunker and work out this mystery."

Fargo had heard that Sagebrush Sadie was a regular hellcat. That she'd fight anyone at the drop of a feather, and drop the feather herself. He was mildly surprised, then, when she abruptly backed down.

"You have a point, I reckon. We need to find out what this is about." Sadie settled herself and Fargo and California and Tom did the same. "I reckon the place to start is with the letters," she began. "I got one from Tennessee, which he says he never sent."

"I honest to God did not," the Southerner said. "Hell, I can barely write a lick." He added sheepishly, "I never had much schoolin'. Pa needed help around the farm."

"I got a letter from Sadie," Jed Crow said. "Which she didn't send."

Each of them spoke up. Each of them had received a letter that the sender claimed never to have mailed.

"It's the damnedest thing I ever heard of," California Jim remarked.

Fargo reached into his pocket and produced the letter

he'd received. Unfolding it, he laid it out flat. "Who here still has theirs?"

It turned out that California, Bear River Tom, and Sadie did. Badger had thrown his away. Tennessee didn't know what had happened to his.

"Let me have them," Fargo directed, and when they handed the letters over, he spread the others out next to his.

"Will you look at that," California Jim said.

"Even I can tell the handwritin' is the same," Tennessee said.

The note on each was to the point: *Need to see you at Fort Carlson by the end of the month. Important you be there.* But each was signed with a different name.

Sagebrush Sadie squatted next to Fargo, her leg brushing his. "The same person sent all of these."

Badger leaned over Fargo's shoulder to say, "It looks the same as the writing that was on mine. Only mine said that I should expect some friends to show up by the end of the month, and for me to stick around. Not that I was going anywhere."

"Someone wants all of us together," Bear River Tom stated the obvious.

"But why?" California wondered.

"If'n it's one of you playin' a joke," Tennessee said, "I ain't amused."

"Me either," Jed Crow said. "I left my wife and kids and came all this way to find out I wasn't really sent for? I find out who did this, I'll plant my boot up their ass."

"Boot, hell," Sagebrush Sadie said, and patted the hilt of her bowie. "I'll shove this so far up, he can use it to shave with."

Fargo had been listening with half an ear while studying the handwriting. The letters were large and uneven, done in a rushed scrawl. "A man wrote this," he deduced.

"Or a gal pretending to be a man," Sagebrush Sadie said.

"It weren't me," Tennessee said. "I write so slow, it'd take me a month of Sundays to just write one letter."

"That doesn't prove anything," Badger said.

"Are you accusin' me?" Tennessee responded.

"If I was," Badger said, "you'd be lying on the ground spitting blood." He straightened and glared at all of them. "This is my post. I don't need nor want any of you here."

"Friendly cuss," California Jim said.

"I don't pretend to be something I'm not."

"I don't know why you're mad at us," Tennessee said, sounding hurt. "We're not to blame."

"If not one of you, then who?" Badger said.

Fargo collected the letters and stood. "I have an idea how we can find out if it was one of us."

"We're listening, pard," California Jim said.

"We go to the fort," Fargo proposed. "Find some paper and a pencil. Each of us writes the same thing as in the letters."

Tennessee snapped his fingers. "I get it. Whoever wrote them will have the same handwritin'."

"And whoever the hell it is," Badger said grimly, "will wish to hell they hadn't."

Bear River Tom chuckled. "Aren't we a friendly bunch? We get some silly letters and we're ready to kill the writer."

"We already know it wasn't you," Fargo said, and cracked a grin.

"How so?" Bear River Tom asked.

"There's no mention of tits."

# 5

The day was sunny and bright, the forest rich with wild-life. Birds sang and squirrels scampered and an incau-tious rabbit panicked and bounded away in high leaps.

Badger rode ahead of everyone else. After him came Jed Crow, Sagebrush Sadie, and Tennessee. Fargo was at the rear with California Jim and Bear River Tom.

"I still say this is a damn silly business," the latter now remarked. "Bringing all of us here for no reason."

California Jim nodded. "As practical jokes go, it's pointless."

"Maybe one of us did it to make Badger mad," Bear River Tom said. "Did you see that look on his face? Why does he hate us being here so much?"

"Like he said, Fort Carlson is his post," California Jim reminded him.

"Even so, it's plumb childish. But then Badger has always been too high-strung. He's always on edge. What he needs is to relax." Bear River Tom grinned lecher-ously. "A night with a nice pair of tits would do him won-ders."

"I knew you'd squeeze tits in there somewhere," Cali-fornia Jim said, and turned to Fargo. "You're awful quiet, pard. No thoughts on this nonsense?"

"Only that it's not."

"I beg your pardon?"

"Nonsense," Fargo said. "Someone went to a lot of trouble. Writing those letters. Mailing them off. They wouldn't do it on a lark."

Bear River Tom scrunched his craggy features. "The

thing I've been wondering about," he said, "is how they knew where to send the things."

Fargo hadn't thought of that. The six of them had been scattered all over creation. Jed Crow would be easiest to reach; everyone knew he lived with the Crows. Tennessee had been working as a scout out of Fort Laramie. California and Tom had been at other forts. Sagebrush Sadie had been spending time enjoying the sights in Denver. And he'd just come back from the Mount Shasta country of northern California.

"It could have been done through the army," California Jim said. "If someone knew how to go through channels."

"Whoever it is must have planned it out in advance," Bear River Tom said.

"Planned *what* out?" California said.

They were the last to emerge from the forest. Badger had gone on ahead toward the fort but Tennessee, Sagebrush Sadie, and Jed Crow had stopped to wait for them.

"We've been talkin' it over," the Southerner said, "and we'd like to head to Salt Creek later."

"Don't you mean the Salt River?" Bear River Tom said, and nodded at the ribbon of water visible beyond Fort Carlson.

"Guess you ain't heard," Tennessee said. "A settlement has sprung up south of here. They call it Salt Creek on account of a creek that flows into the river."

"There's too much Salt in these parts," Bear River Tom said.

"Not another damn settlement?" California said. "I swear, ten more years and we'll have as many people west of the Mississippi River as there are east of it."

"I don't like it either," Sagebrush Sadie said. "I hope I don't live to see the West become civilized."

Fargo shared her sentiment. He loved the wild places, loved to roam the mountains and the prairies and the deserts. But bit by bit, year by year, they were losing a little of their wildness. Prairie grass was churned under the plow. Woodland was chopped down to build with.

Settlements and towns and even a few cities had become hubs for more.

"What I'd like to know—" Jed Crow started, and he suddenly grunted and wrenched sideways in his saddle.

For a few seconds the rest of them were riveted in place by the sight of an arrow that had thudded into Crow's chest.

Fargo recovered first. He reined around and drew his Colt as another feathered shaft streaked out of the undergrowth. It missed Tennessee's coonskin cap by inches, and only because the Southerner had chosen that moment to hunch low over his saddle.

"Injuns!" Tennessee bawled.

Fargo fired at the spot the arrow came from, and jabbed his spurs. He reined right and then left to make himself harder to hit. Flying in among the pines, he spied a figure racing away. A figure with long black hair and a buckskin shirt and leggings and moccasins.

A young face painted for war glanced back at him, and the warrior ran faster.

A second warrior broke cover, joining the first in flight.

Fargo was so intent on catching them that he almost took an arrow, when a third silhouette rose from concealment, a shaft notched to a sinew string.

Shifting, Fargo fired at the center of the darkling shape. He scored, too; the shape staggered and the bow fell.

Then Fargo was past and turning to shoot at the others but someone beat him to it.

Emmett Badger had been farthest away but now he was close behind the Ovaro. His mare was so swift, he'd outraced the others. And it was Badger, a Colt in his hand, who fired two shots as quick as anything.

The second warrior folded in on himself and collapsed into a tumble.

The first warrior, the one who had put an arrow into Jed Crow, plunged into a thicket.

Fargo rode around to the other side but didn't see him. He went another twenty yards, then hauled on the reins and rose in the stirrups.

The thick undergrowth could hide fifty warriors.

Another heartbeat, and Emmett Badger brought his mare to a sliding stop next to the Ovaro. "Where?"

Fargo, still searching, shook his head.

"We hunt him," Badger said, and reined to the right.

Fargo reined left. He must have covered an acre when hooves drummed and California Jim and Bear River Tom galloped up on either side.

"Any sign?" California asked.

Fargo's scowl was his answer.

"Damned redskins," Bear River Tom said. "We should go see about Crow."

"Not yet," Fargo said, and went on searching. Only when he was convinced the war party was gone did he turn back.

The others promptly followed suit.

"A hell of a note," California Jim said. "We should have been on our guard. The colonel warned us about the renegades."

"I didn't think they'd strike this close to the fort," Bear River Tom justified their lapse.

"We were too caught up in those damn letters," California Jim said.

The brush crackled, and all three of them brought guns to bear.

Out of it came Emmett Badger. "Nothing," he said before they could ask. "The sons of bitches got clean away."

"We'll find them," California Jim said. "Sooner or later."

"Hell, we're the best scouts alive," Bear River Tom threw in. "If we can't, no one can."

Jed Crow was on his back on the ground, Sagebrush Sadie on her knees beside him, holding his hand in both of hers.

She looked up as they came to a stop. "Tennessee went to the fort for the sawbones."

"How is he?" California asked.

Sadie gave a barely perceptible shake of her head.

"Why haven't you taken the arrow out?" Bear River Tom asked.

Fargo could see why from where he sat. The shaft was too close to Crow's heart. Dismounting, he walked over and dipped to a knee.

Jed Crow was conscious. Drops of blood flecked his lips, and a wet stain covered half his shirt. "Stupid way to die," he said, and coughed. It brought more blood, in rivulets.

"You might want to lie still," Fargo advised.

"Do me a favor," Crow said. "Get word to my missus. Her name is Bright Star."

"Which band is it?" Fargo couldn't recollect if he'd ever been told.

"The Ashalaho," Jed Crow said. "Do you know where to find them?"

Fargo nodded. He'd been through Crow country many a time. He'd even been with a Crow woman or three; they were fine as could be under a bear hide at night. "I'll see it's done."

"I'm obliged," Crow said, and broke into another, more violent, fit. When he subsided he was pasty with sweat, and gasping. "Not long now."

"Is there anything I can get you?" Sadie asked. "Anything I can do for you?"

"I never should have come," Crow said weakly. "Never should have left my family." He clutched at the arrow, and groaned.

"I've got a flask," California remarked, and reached back to a saddlebag.

"Be a waste of whiskey," Crow said. His chin was scarlet, his breathing labored. "Did you get the one who killed me?"

"Not yet," Bear River Tom said, "but we sure as hell won't stop looking."

"I give you my word," Emmett Badger said, "he's as good as dead."

Jed Crow gazed skyward. "God. I'll never see my kids

again." His eyes filled with tears. "That's the hardest part."

California cleared his throat and looked away, and pointed toward the fort. "Tennessee and some soldier boys are on their way."

"Too late," Crow said, and coughed. "The sawbones won't get here in time to do any good."

"I'm so sorry," Sagebrush Sadie said softly.

"You're a good gal, Sadie," Crow said. "Remember when we met at Fort Leavenworth? It must have been ten years ago. You said as how one day you'd be—" Crow stopped, and his eyes widened.

"Jed?" Sadie said.

"It's the end of me," Crow said. He exhaled once, and was gone.

"Damn," Sadie said, bowing her head.

Using two fingers, Fargo closed Crow's glazing eyes. "I'll see to the burying."

"I'll help, pard," California Jim offered.

Bear River Tom leaned on his saddle horn. "And now there are six of us."

# 6

Colonel Carlson sent out a patrol to scour the valley for sign of the hostiles, then had the scouts file into his office and demanded they give his or her account of Jed Crow's death.

Fargo thought it was high-handed but he went along since the others did.

The colonel had Sagebrush Sadie start things off—"Ladies first"—and then each of them in turn. Fargo happened to be seated in the last chair on the left and Carlson called on him last.

"We're about done. Let's hear your report."

"Bannocks jumped us. Jed Crow took an arrow. He died."

Colonel Carlson waited half a minute for more and when there was none he tilted his head and said, "That's it?"

"Except for the part where your sawbones got there and pronounced Crow dead."

"The others gave more detailed versions," Colonel Carlson said. "Perhaps you would like to flesh out yours so we don't miss anything."

"We haven't missed a goddamn thing," Fargo said.

"I told you before. I don't much like the tone you take with me."

Fargo knew better but he said, "I don't give a damn. You've kept us here for over an hour now, asking the same questions and getting the same answers. There's nothing more we can tell you."

"How about if you let me be the judge of that?"

"How about I don't." Fargo stood and touched his hat brim. "Thanks for the hospitality."

Carlson went rigid with suppressed anger. "You're not going anywhere unless I give permission."

"Want to bet?" Fargo started toward the door.

"Stop right there. I can have you thrown in the guardhouse with Lone Bear for failing to cooperate."

Wheeling, Fargo marched to the desk, placed both hands flat, and leaned toward Carlson until their faces were practically touching. "No," he said, "you can't. I'm not in the army's employ at the moment. I'm a civilian, and you have no damn say over civilians unless they're breaking federal law."

"This is *my* post—"

Fargo gestured, cutting Carlson off. "And I'm sure General Decker will love to hear how you run it."

"Decker?" Carlson said, and blinked.

California Jim cleared his throat and commented, "My pard has done scouting for a lot of the top brass. He's good friends with more than a few who wear stars on their shoulders. Hell, he even met Abe Lincoln, himself, once."

Colonel Carlson spread his hands. "Look. You shot one of the hostiles. You must have been close enough to get a good look at the others who got away."

Fargo straightened.

"If I took you to their village, could you identify them?"

"No," Fargo lied. He wouldn't forget the one who had killed Jed Crow.

"Very well, then. You may go," Carlson said with obvious reluctance. "But should you give me any more trouble, I'll ban you from the fort. Friends in high places, or not." He smiled a resentful smile.

"Fine by me," Fargo said, and got the hell out of there. He was halfway to the Ovaro when the others caught up.

"What in tarnation was that all about, pard?" California Jim asked. "You lit into him like a bobcat into a wood rat."

"He had it coming."

Bear River Tom chuckled. "I know what you need. A nice big pair of tits to help you simmer down."

Fargo tried counting to ten in his head.

"That will be enough about tits in the presence of a lady," Sagebrush Sadie said.

"What are you so touchy about?" Bear River Tom responded. "You see a pair every day."

"Here now," Tennessee said. "I won't have you talkin' to her like that."

Their budding spat was clipped short by Emmett Badger, who suddenly was in front of Fargo, fists bunched.

"You're in my way," Fargo said.

"I don't like what you did in there," Badger said. "Carlson is my commanding officer."

"How nice for you," Fargo said, and shouldered past. He'd taken a couple of steps when Badger's hand fell on his shoulder and spun him around.

"Don't walk off on me," Badger said. "I wasn't done."

"You are now," Fargo said, and hit him, a short, swift uppercut that rocked the other scout onto his heels but didn't drop him as it would most men.

Badger took a step back, gave his head a shake, and put a hand to his chin. "I owe you for that."

"Here and now is fine."

"No," Badger said. "The colonel would throw us both in the guardhouse. I'll pick the time and the place." Wheeling, he stalked off.

"That was uncalled for," Sadie said.

"Badger put his hand on him." Bear River Tom came to Fargo's defense. "I'd have done the same thing."

"Oh, please," Sadie said. "None of us would dare rile Badger except him." She nodded at Fargo.

"Give him cause," California Jim chuckled, "and my pard will rile just about anybody."

"Listen to all of you," Tennessee said in disgust. "We just lost Jed Crow, and here you all are squabblin' like a passel of kids."

That shut them up.

Fargo stepped to the Ovaro, forked leather, and reined to the south, glancing back once at the guardhouse.

Lone Bear's face was at the bars, watching. Their eyes met. "Hell," Fargo said to himself, and tapped his spurs.

He preferred to be alone but it wasn't to be. He hadn't gone a hundred yards when he acquired a shadow on his right.

"Mind telling me what that was all about?" California Jim asked.

"You were there."

"I know you have slim patience with idiots, but still."

"Some days I don't have any."

California Jim sighed. "Well, good riddance to Fort Carlson, then. Let's head elsewhere and forget this whole mess."

"Can't," Fargo said.

California Jim stared a considerable spell and then said, "Tell me you're not thinking what I think you're thinking."

"It's not right and you know it."

"What are the Bannocks to us? Have you met Lone Bear before?"

"No."

"Then why in hell stir up the blue hornets? I could savvy if he was a friend."

"You've lived with Indians, the same as me," Fargo said. "A chief can't be held to account for warriors who don't do as he wants."

"I know, I know," California said.

"Well, then," Fargo said.

"Carlson will want to carve your gizzard out. Badger won't be too happy, neither."

"There's another reason we can't leave yet," Fargo said. "Those letters."

"They have to be a practical joke. Why else would anyone want to trick all of us into coming here, of all places?"

"I'd like to find out."

"Uh-oh," California Jim said. "I know that look. You're fixing to push and prod until you get answers."

"First things first," Fargo said.

"First we go to that new settlement and get so drunk we can't hardly sit straight?"

"We do."

"If you were female, I'd marry you," California Jim said.

As settlements went, Salt Creek was pathetic. A gob of spit was bigger. But it had a saloon, and even if whoever painted the sign spelled saloon with one "o," it was a whiskey mill, and that was all that counted.

Fargo pushed through the batwings and strode over to the bar. The few locals playing cards or drinking paid them no mind. Smacking the counter, he said, "Monongahela. And leave the bottle."

"Yes, sir." In his previous life the bartender might have been a mouse. He timidly brought a bottle over and set it down as if he expected to be attacked. "Something the matter, mister?"

"Why do you ask?"

The mouse indicated the mirror behind the bar.

Fargo hadn't realized it, but his face resembled a thundercloud about to burst. "Having one of those days," he said.

"Oh," the man said, and some of the worry went out of him. "I have them myself. It always makes me want to go back to bed."

"Makes me want to shoot someone." Fargo tilted the bottle and gulped. Familiar and welcome warmth spread clear down to his toes, and he smiled in contentment and let out an "Ahhhh."

The bartender took that as a good sign. "No watered-down bug juice here. You get what you pay for."

"This place have any law?" Fargo asked.

The man snorted. "Hell, we don't even have a mayor. Or a council. The army sort of keeps an eye on things but they can't really do much." He paused. "Why? Are you expecting trouble?"

"The day I've been having," Fargo said, and let it go at that.

California Jim bellied up beside him. "How's the coffin varnish? Good enough to pickle my innards?"

"It will do some fine pickling," Fargo assured him.

"Sadie and Tom and Tennessee followed us," California mentioned. "They're coming up the street."

"Figured they would," Fargo said.

"Someone else is with them."

"Figured there would be."

"So soon?" California said.

"He's not the kind to let grass grow under him. He'll want to get it over with."

"You were on the prod, you know. You could maybe apologize," California suggested.

"Has hell froze over?" Fargo returned. He was raising the glass when the batwings parted yet again and into the "salon" came Bear River Tom and Sagebrush Sadie and the lanky Tennessean.

And Emmett Badger.

# 7

Badger didn't hesitate or stop or bluster. He stalked across the room and planted himself in front of Fargo. "I don't need to say why."

"No," Fargo said, "you don't."

"We've shared drinks but we have it to do."

"Then stop jabbering and get on with it," Fargo said, setting the bottle down.

"A man after my own heart." Emmett Badger smiled, and struck with the blinding speed of a rattler.

Fargo saw the punch coming and tried to jerk aside but Badger was ungodly quick. Knuckles as hard as stone caught him flush on the jaw and knocked him against the bar. He retaliated with a left but Badger blocked and drove a fist into his gut. He grunted and doubled over, his vision swimming. He braced for another blow but none came.

Shaking his head, he could see again.

Badger had taken a couple of steps back and raised his fists. "I thought you'd be tougher."

Sadie had a hand to her throat. Bear River Tom seemed to be amused. Tennessee was leaning on his long rifle, clearly unhappy at the turn of events.

"Waiting for Christmas?" Badger taunted.

"No pistols, no knives."

"Fine by me."

"No biting ears off."

"What?"

"I heard about the fight you had with that soldier at Fort Bridger."

"It was only one ear."

"I don't give a damn. No biting ears. Noses, neither."

"Well, hell." Badger scowled. "Is this a fight or a church social? Next you'll be saying I can't kick you in the balls."

"Kicking in the balls is fine," Fargo said, and kicked Badger in the balls.

Badger tried to skip out of the way but Fargo's boot caught him where it would hurt the most. Badger colored and backpedaled.

Now it was Fargo's turn to taunt. "Are you sure you have any? They must be as big as marbles."

Badger snarled like his namesake and waded in with his fists flying.

Fargo had been in a lot of fights in his time. California Jim said his disposition had a lot to do with it. Fargo liked to think it was because there were too many jackasses in the world. Whatever the reason, he had a lot of experience at trading punches, and he needed all of it to hold his own against Emmett Badger. The man met him blow for blow, and then some. In no time he realized he was in for a lollapalooza.

Badger's reputation was well earned. He punched like a giant and absorbed punches like a sponge.

Fargo rammed a right that would fold most men in half but all Badger did was grunt and retaliate with a left that nearly broke Fargo's jaw.

Over by the front window, Bear River Tom let out with a loud, "Wahooooo! We're having fun now!"

Fargo reminded himself that some simpletons were more simple than others, and paid for being distracted with a fist to his cheek that snapped his head back. Gritting his teeth, he whipped a cross at Badger's face but Badger blocked and countered with a punch to his ribs that Fargo swore damn near cracked it.

Sagebrush Sadie hollered, "Stop it, you two! Before someone gets hurt!"

Too late for that, Fargo reflected, and slammed Badger on the temple. Badger staggered, shook himself, and became a whirlwind of feet and hands.

Fargo blocked or avoided most of the blows. A boot slammed his shin and a fist creased his jaw and then a fist tried to drive his navel out his spine. It bent him over and put his jaw right where Badger wanted it.

The room seemed to explode. The next Fargo was aware, he was on his butt on the floor, and the bar and the tables and chairs were spinning around and around. He closed his eyes and the spinning continued inside his head.

"Had enough?"

Fargo glanced up. "Not while I'm breathing."

"Suit yourself. But I'm not holding back anymore."

"Makes two of us," Fargo said, and was on his feet with his blood boiling.

They joined again, slugging with no quarter asked, fists landing with brutal force.

Fargo lost sight of everyone and everything except Emmett Badger. He was conscious only of throwing punches and being punched. Then Badger's arm lowered, just a fraction, but it was enough.

Now it was Badger who was on the floor wearing a dazed look. "Damn," he said. "Are there three of you or is it me?"

"There are three of me," Fargo said, "and we'll stomp the hell out of you if you get back up."

"You know I will."

"Damn it. Let's call a truce."

"You shouldn't have hit me back at the fort."

"I agree. I should have hit Carlson."

"Apology accepted," Badger said, slowly rising. "And count yourself lucky."

Fargo moved to the bar and reached for his bottle. "Let's drink to our bruises."

"You hit like a goddamn sledgehammer."

The others came over, Sadie shaking her head and Tennessee making "tsk-tsk" sounds.

"Are we to take it the hostilities are over?" California Jim asked.

"They are," Fargo said. "I'm about to drink him under the table."

"Dream on," Badger said.

"Men," Sadie said.

"Tits," Bear River Tom said.

Both Fargo and Badger stared at him, and Badger said, "Pass the bottle, would you?"

California Jim bent and picked up something from the floor. He examined it, then held it out to Badger. "Here. I believe this is yours."

It was a tooth.

"Hell," Badger said, and touched his jaw.

"I saw it fly out of your mouth when he clipped you a good one."

"Oh well. I got plenty left."

California pointed at Fargo's ear. "And you might want to get that stitched or you'll have a scar."

Fargo reached up. To say his ear was mangled was being charitable. "Well, damn."

"I hope you two are satisfied with your antics," Sagebrush Sadie said. "Making a spectacle of yourselves like that."

The bartender coughed. "It was the best fight we ever had in here. No one broke anything."

"Did anyone ask you?" Sadie snapped.

"No ma'am."

"Then keep your two bits to yourself or you and me will go at it."

"Go at it how, ma'am? With pillows or fists?"

"Say pillows again and I will by-God shoot you."

"Scouts," the bartender said. "Prickly as cactus."

That struck Fargo as funny. He started to laugh, and Badger started to laugh, and in another moment the two of them were cackling.

"You two whale the tar out of each other," Bear River Tom said, "and then act like it's no different than squeezing a pair of "—he caught himself and finished with—"cow's teats."

"You're lucky you said cow," Sagebrush Sadie said.

"What do cows have to do with this?" the bartender wanted to know.

"God, this is ridiculous," Badger said.

"I'll drink to that," Fargo said.

Sadie was glaring at the barkeep. "Who asked you to keep butting in?"

"Why are you biting my head off?" the bartender whined. "I'm not your husband."

"Oh, good one," Bear River Tom said.

"Is it me," Tennessee said, "or are all of you half loco?"

"Probably more than half," California Jim said.

"I feel like I'm in an asylum," the bartender said.

"And to think," California Jim said, "none of us are drunk yet."

Fargo gulped Monongahela and held out the bottle to Badger.

"Obliged," the other scout said, and fastened his mouth to it.

"Save some for me," California Jim requested.

"Fighters first," Fargo said.

Sadie snorted. "If men ever make sense, the world will come to an end."

"It already has for Jed Crow," Tennessee reminded them.

That killed the good mood.

California paid for a second bottle and they passed it back and forth.

"Once we're so drunk we can't pee in a pot without help," Bear River Tom brought up, along about his fourth swig, "what then?"

"I'm headin' for Fort Laramie," Tennessee said.

"It's Denver for me once this is done," Sadie said. "I have business to attend to."

"Man business?" Bear River Tom said, and leered and winked.

"How about I blow your peter off?" Sadie said.

Tom cocked his head. "What's with you, woman? You're always talking about shooting a man in his Rocky Mountain oysters."

"I didn't say your oysters," Sadie replied. "I said pecker and I meant pecker."

*41*

"Spoken like a true lady," Bear River Tom said. "Next you'll be wearing a dress and joining a sewing circle."

"Uh-oh," Tennessee said.

Bear River Tom was smirking at his jest and likely didn't see Sadie let fly or he'd have avoided the fist that caught him on the jaw. He bleated and took a couple of steps back and she went after him. She could fight, too. She held her fists as a boxer would and jabbed and flicked solid rights and lefts.

"At it again," the bartender said. "I should charge folks to watch."

"Tom will make mincemeat of her," California Jim said. "He's five times her size."

But Tom wasn't trying to hit her, only to stop her from hitting him.

Tennessee cupped a hand to his mouth and hollered, "That's it, Sadie gal. You can lick him."

"Anytime she wants," Bear River Tom managed to say while ducking and twisting. "I like tongue almost as much as I like tits."

Sadie hopped into the air and kicked at his privates. Her aim was off and she buried her foot in his belly.

"That hurt," Tom said.

It was then that a man covered with blood lurched through the batwings.

# 8

The man took a few staggering steps, cried out, "Massacre!" and pitched to the floor.

Fargo and Badger were the first to reach him. Fargo sank to a knee and together they carefully rolled him over.

"Butchers," Badger said.

It looked like someone had used the man for chopping practice; his body, his arms, his legs, bore dozens of slash marks. Some were shallow. Some were deep. His clothes were soaked red.

"I know that fella," one of the locals declared. "His name is Johnson. He has a place about half a mile up the creek."

"Farmer?" Bear River Tom said.

"Hunter," the local answered. "He's got a cabin off in the backwoods. Him and his family."

"Family," Sadie said, and blanched.

The backwoodsman's eyes fluttered open. He had to try twice to croak, "Got hold of her . . ."

"Who got hold of who, mister?" California Jim asked when the man didn't go on.

"My girl," the backwoodsman said. "She . . . she's only ten."

"Was it the Bannocks?" Tennessee asked.

"Think so," the man gasped.

"Who else would it be?" California said. "This is Bannock country."

"My boys. Little Sophie," the man said. "My wife . . ." He looked at the ceiling, arched his back, and keened,

"Why, God? What did we do? Tell me why?" His eyes closed, he shuddered, and folded in on himself and was still.

"Maybe he'll get his answer on the other side," California Jim said.

"Or maybe he's just dead," Bear River Tom said.

"The Bible says different," Tennessee said.

Sadie looked at them as if she couldn't believe what she was hearing. "Didn't you hear him about his girl? Why are we still here?"

Fargo was up and outside before any of them and reached the horses a couple of strides ahead of Badger.

Word was already spreading, and the settlement's inhabitants were hurrying from their homes and businesses to converge on the saloon.

"I told the barkeep to get word to the fort," California Jim said.

"It'll be a couple of hours before any soldiers get here, I reckon," Tennessee said. "Bluebellies are turtles."

"We're not," Fargo said. He reined down the street and over to the creek and headed up it.

Badger quickly caught up. "Damn stupid settlers," he said.

Fargo agreed. The dead man was a fool to take his family off so deep into the woods. Back East it would be fine. Back East most hostile tribes had been exterminated or forced onto reservations. But this was the West, where many tribes hated the whites for trying to do to them as the whites had done to those others.

Truth told, Fargo's sympathies were with the Indians. His own kind were locusts, taking over everything in their path. That he was helping the locusts pricked at his conscience now and again. But he liked scouting more than any other work and aimed to keep at it until the day he died.

The others soon were right behind them, the drum of their horses' hooves rumbling like thunder.

Fargo remembered the ambush near the fort, and

stayed alert. When they had gone about four miles, he slowed.

"What are you're doing?" Sadie demanded.

"Think, gal," Tennessee said. "It could be the war party is still there."

"But the little girl . . ." Sadie said.

Fargo felt the same urgency. But it wouldn't do to ride into a hail of arrows, and he said so.

"I know," Sadie said. "I just hate it when it's kids, is all."

"Same here, gal," California Jim said. "Them as will hurt children, red or white, are scum."

Bear River Tom remarked, "They'll probably take her back to their village and raise her as one of their own and in ten years she'll be married to some buck and be raising a pack of half-breeds."

Sadie gave him a withering glance.

"What's the matter with you?" Tom asked.

"Hush up," Fargo said. He'd be damned if he'd listen to another petty argument.

"My God, you people are touchy," Bear River Tom muttered loud enough that everyone heard.

"I thought you don't believe in Him?" California said.

"When I say hush," Fargo broke in, "I really mean shut your damn mouths."

The family had worn a track in their comings and goings from the settlement. It led around the next bend to a wide clearing.

Fargo drew rein.

"Oh, hell," Tennessee said.

The cabin door was open and most every article the family owned had been brought out and smashed and torn and scattered willy-nilly. Amid the debris lay bodies: a woman and a small boy, mother and son, her arm protectively over him, both mutilated. An older boy lay off toward the outhouse, his shirt ripped open, his flesh peeled to the spine. A dog, the head attached by a sliver of skin and fur, was near him. Even the chickens had been killed, their heads chopped off.

"You'd think they'd take the birds to eat," Bear River Tom said.

Fargo alighted and palmed his Colt. The stillness suggested the war party was gone but they could just as well be lying in ambush. He went to the woman and the small boy. There was no need to bend down and examine them. "Hell," he said.

"Same with this one," California Jim said from over by the outhouse.

"Find the sign," Badger said.

They spread out. It wasn't a minute later that Tennessee, who had drifted to the northeast, hunkered and hollered, "They skedaddled this-a-way."

Everyone joined him.

The tracks were plain, and the horses weren't shod.

"I reckon ten or more," Tennessee said. "Likely headin' back to their village."

"We're wasting time," Sadie said.

Fargo and Badger assumed the lead. For over a mile the depth and spacing of the tracks showed that the war party had fled at a gallop. Eventually the warriors had slowed, convinced no one was after them.

"I hope we take them by surprise," Bear River Tom observed, "and take a few alive so we can do to them like they did to those settlers."

"We kill as many as we can, as quick as we can," Badger said.

"Why can't we have some fun while we're at it?" Bear River Tom rejoined.

"I wonder if any have guns," Tennessee said. "I'd rather go against bows."

"Bows they learned to use as soon as they learned to walk," California Jim said. "Don't ever underestimate an Injun with a bow."

"We should have an edge with our rifles," Tennessee insisted.

"Tell that to Jed Crow," was California Jim's rebuttal.

"Biddy hens," Fargo said, and clucked to the Ovaro.

He'd never realized it before, but put a bunch of scouts together and they acted like a ladies' sewing circle.

Once again Badger stayed alongside him. "Doesn't this strike you as a mite too easy?"

"They're on horseback," Fargo said.

"Even so," Badger said, "they're not making any effort to throw us off."

"If you're right," Fargo said, "they'll pick the best spot they can." He motioned at the peaks and slopes that stretched to the horizon. "You've been at the post a spell. Know this area?"

"I've been through it," Badger said. "The Bannocks know it a lot better."

"Remind the others to keep their eyes skinned."

"You think they don't know that?"

"Remind them anyway."

Badger went to rein around, and paused. "I'm the official scout here. I should be giving the orders."

"You are."

Badger went back down the line.

Fargo shucked the Henry from the saddle scabbard and held it across his saddle, ready for quick use. When the attack came they'd be lucky to have a split-second's warning.

Another mile, and another horse was beside the Ovaro.

"I hate this," Sagebrush Sadie said. "I hate it when a family is involved."

"You see anyone jumping for joy?"

"I have a soft spot for children. Always have. I suppose because I've never had any of my own."

"What's stopping you?" Fargo said. "You have the equipment for it."

A pink blush crept into Sadie's cheeks. "I'd expect that from Tom but not from you. And how the hell could I raise a kid, traipsing all over creation like I do?"

"If you ever find the right man, odds are you'll settle down."

"Listen to you," Sadie said. "I don't see you hitched."

"And you never will."

"With my luck," Sadie said, "the man who claims my heart won't want a family. All he'll be interested in is killing and whatnot."

"Why in hell would someone want to do that?" Fargo asked.

Sadie shrugged. "My problem is the same as yours and most of these others."

"Oh?"

"We're alike, us scouts," Sadie said. "Wanderlust is in our blood. We go where the wind blows us."

"You have me pegged," Fargo said.

"Of course I do. Just because I'm female doesn't mean I must have some peculiar female reason for being a scout. I do it because I love it." Sadie paused. "When I can."

"What's that mean?"

"It's harder for me than it is for you and the rest of them."

"Because you have to squat when you pee?"

"Damn it, I'm serious," Sadie said, but she chuckled. "No, it's harder because there are a lot of officers who won't have anything to do with a female scout. They think because I'm female I can't be as good as a male."

Fargo was about to say that based on what he'd heard, she was as good as any scout alive, when Bear River Tom called out a warning.

"The Bannocks!"

# 9

Fargo drew rein and whipped the Henry to his shoulder but not so much as a single war whoop shattered the serenity of the forest and no arrows sought his hide.

"Up there," Bear River Tom said, pointing.

Half a mile higher reared a ridge partly in timber and partly open. Strung out in single file, a line of riders was just about to cross over to the other side.

"Consarn you, Tom, you lunkhead," Tennessee said. "I thought we were about to be attacked."

"So did I," California Jim said. "Good thing we're too far away for them to hear you."

"Doesn't matter," Badger said. "They know we're here. They wanted us to see them."

"Luring us in, huh?" Tennessee said.

Fargo kept going, his eyes on the ridge. He forgot about Sadie until she gave a slight cough.

"As I was saying, it's a lot harder for me than it is for the rest of you."

Fargo hardly thought this was the time or place to talk about their profession. There might be warriors lying in wait on the way up, arrows nocked to pick them off.

"It's hard for women all over," Sadie rambled on. "There aren't as many jobs for us as there are for you, and those there are bore me to hell. Work as a seamstress? Sit in a chair all day sewing? I'd rather slit my wrists than live so dull a life."

Fargo grunted to pretend he gave a damn.

"A lot of women are cooks. But who wants to sweat at a hot stove eight to ten hours a day? I sure as hell don't."

Fargo grunted again. A man could say a lot with a grunt.

"There's cleaning, and being a maid, and such," Sadie said. "But it'll be a cold day in hell before I scrub someone else's floors. And could you see me prancing around in a maid outfit?"

Fargo imagined the shapely body under her buckskins. "That would be something. You're easy on the eyes."

"Why, thank you, kind sir," Sadie said, and blushed. "But no. Being a maid calls for a lot of kowtowing, and 'yes, sir' and 'no, ma'am.' I don't lick boots. Never have, never will."

"Is there a point to all this?"

"It's the same point as before," Sadie said. "The only kind of work I like is scouting. I was a tomboy when I was young, and I reckon spending my days in the woods hunting and fishing and exploring got into my bones."

Fargo would like to get into her pants but didn't say so.

"So it's scouting or nothing. The problem is, not enough take me serious."

"I do," Fargo said. He'd always held that women could do most any job a man could. Female muleskinners and stage drivers and a lady doc he'd met confirmed his belief.

"Why, thank you," Sadie said, and blushed anew. "I wish more army officers were like you. And those who hire pilots for the wagon trains to Oregon country and wherever."

"You have to try harder than men," Fargo said, thinking that if he showed her he understood, she'd shut the hell up.

"You don't know the half of it. Half the time I have to practically beg to get work. Why, down to New Mexico, they needed a scout to lead a patrol into Apache country. I happened to be there and volunteered. But would they let me? No. A major looked me right in the eye and told me it was no work for a female." Sadie swore. "I could have shot him."

"You might have Bannocks to shoot soon," Fargo said, hoping she would take the hint.

"No," Sadie said sadly, "being a woman in a man's world is no picnic. A girl who wants to get ahead on her own has to resort to all sorts of tricks."

"Such as?" Fargo absently asked.

"Oh, I won't say. But the things I've had to do." Sadie paused. "I can't ever do enough, though. The year before last I worked five months out of the twelve. Ain't that pitiful?"

Fargo was growing irritated.

"I'm tired of hardly ever having enough to buy the supplies I need or for ammunition or to have my horse shoed. I want more work, damn it, and I will by-God have it."

"I'll see what I can do about sending some your way," Fargo said, and gigged the Ovaro to pull ahead and nip further babble in the bud. He was following a game trail, the same trail the Bannocks had used.

The trail entered a belt of firs, the trees so high and so close together that they were plunged in perpetual shadow.

It was as good a spot for an ambush as any, and a feeling came over him, a feeling he'd had before. Some part of him, deep down, knew that as surely as the sun rose in the east and set in the west, a few of the Bannocks were in the firs, waiting.

Twisting in the saddle, Fargo said quietly to Sagebrush Sadie, "They're fixing to jump us. Pass it along."

Sadie gave a mild start, and slowed so she was next to California Jim.

Fargo shoved the Henry into the scabbard and palmed his Colt. In the narrow ranks of firs, the short gun was better.

A heavy silence had fallen, like a cemetery at midnight when there was no wind. The trees, and their branches, were completely still. It was as if the forest was holding its breath, waiting for something to happen.

At times there were aisles between the ranks but then Fargo would come to a cluster so tightly spaced he had to go around. And it was as he was going around one that a sharp cry split the stillness, behind him, and a rifle boomed.

Fargo jabbed his spurs and wheeled to join the others.

They had drawn rein and were scanning the trees with their rifles and pistols trained.

All save for the crumpled form of Tennessee. The Southerner had been last in line and had taken an arrow in the back. He was on his side, thrashing and clutching in vain at the shaft, blood gushing from his mouth.

It was Badger who got to him and vaulted from his mare.

Fargo started to go past Sadie and spotted a shadowed figure with a bow to his left. Swiveling, he fanned the Colt twice and saw the figure rock to the impact and go down.

War whoops shattered the firs as more figures appeared and arrows whizzed.

Bear River Tom fired.

So did California Jim.

Badger, on a knee beside Tennessee, banged off two shots as swiftly as Fargo had done.

A painted warrior charged out of the trees with an upraised tomahawk. He came straight at the Ovaro, his features contorted in hate.

Fargo shot him in the face. He drew rein beside Badger and Tennessee to cover them.

A harsh whinny heralded the crash of Bear River Tom's horse. He scrambled clear, cursing lustily.

And then, just like that, it was over.

The war whoops died. The shadowy figures melted away.

Fargo stayed in the saddle. It could be a trick. It could be the Bannocks had gone to ground and were snaking closer.

A couple of minutes went by and the firs stayed still.

Fargo deemed it safe to climb down. To the rest he said, "Keep your eyes skinned."

Blood trickled from Tennessee's nose as well as his mouth. He was breathing, if barely. His eyes, pools of shock and regret, found Fargo's.

"I reckon this is it," he said.

Badger was examining where the arrow had gone into Tennessee's back. "I can try to dig this out."

"I don't have that long," Tennessee said.

The others were forming a protective ring with their mounts.

"Of all the places to die, this isn't where I'd choose," Tennessee said.

"We don't get to pick," Badger said.

"Try to make him comfortable," Sadie requested.

"How?" Badger returned.

California Jim bent down. "Would you care for some whiskey?"

A weak smile curled Tennessee's thin lips. "I surely would."

It took only a moment for California to rummage his flask from his saddlebag. He opened it and passed it to Fargo who gave it to Badger. Badger cradled Tennessee's head and let him take a sip.

"You're a right fine gentleman," the Southerner said, and coughed.

"I'm so sorry," Sagebrush Sadie said. She appeared about to burst into tears.

"You and me both," Tennessee said.

"I have always liked you," Sadie said. "You've been a good friend."

"Pretty soon now I'll be a dead one." Tennessee coughed, and out spurted more blood.

"Maybe you shouldn't talk," Sadie told him.

"What else do I have to do?" Tennessee closed his eyes, and groaned. "Tarnation, it hurts."

"I could put you out of your misery," Badger offered.

Fargo and everyone else looked at him.

"No, thanks," Tennessee said. "I'll take what I have left."

"What a thing to say," Sadie said to Badger. "He's not a horse with a broke leg."

"No," Badger said, "he's a man and he's suffering. You'll kill a horse that's in a lot of pain but you won't do the same for a man?"

Tennessee looked up. "Tell me you got the one who got me."

"He might have gotten away," Bear River Tom said.

"Some friends you are."

"I'll hunt him down," Badger said. "I'll hunt all of them down."

"You'd do that for me?"

"Not for just you. No one tries to kill me and goes on breathing," Badger said. To stress his point, he repeated, "No one."

"A man after my own heart." Tennessee shook, and gasped. "I'm cold all of a sudden."

Fargo was keeping an eye on the firs, just in case. He appeared to be the only one doing so.

"Is there anyone we can get word to?" California Jim asked. "Kin and such?"

"I only got my ma and two sisters," Tennessee said. "When I don't show in a year or so, they'll know." He grit his teeth. "Won't be long now," he said, and his chest stopped rising and falling.

"Well, hell," California said.

"Now there's only five of us," Bear River Tom said.

# 10

An argument broke out.

Sagebrush Sadie insisted they take Tennessee to the settlement and bury him "proper." California Jim thought that was a waste of time. Bear River Tom agreed with Sadie.

"Listen to all of you," Badger said. "You're forgetting the girl the Bannocks took." He climbed on his mare. "Take the body back if you want but I'm going to get that girl or die trying."

"Makes two of us," Fargo said.

"I make it three," California Jim said.

Bear River Tom looked from them to Sadie and back again. "She shouldn't ought to do it herself."

"I can manage," Sadie said.

"What if Bannocks have circled around and jump you?" Tom said.

Unlikely, Fargo reckoned. Yet he said to Tom, "You go with her. The rest of us will go on."

"I feel bad leaving you," Bear River Tom said.

"Time's a-wasting," Badger declared, and lashed his mare.

Fargo and California rode together. Neither spoke until they were close to the top of the ridge, and had slowed.

"I don't like this, pard," California said. "First Jed, now Tennessee. It's as if someone is out to get us."

"Someone is," Fargo said. "The Bannocks."

"Two of the best scouts alive, done in on the same day."

"We go when we go."

"If I didn't know better, I'd swear someone put a hoo-doo on us."

"But you do know better," Fargo said. "And since when did you become superstitious?"

California shrugged. "Luck can turn against a person. You must know that, all the poker you play."

"Do you want to turn back?"

"No," California said, without a lot of conviction. "We have to do what we can for the little girl."

"Glad you agree."

"Don't be spiteful. My gut is in a knot. Last time I felt this way was that time I took an Apache arrow. Just like Crow and Tennessee."

"You lived. They didn't."

"Damn it. You could show some concern. I forget how hard you can be."

Badger had drawn rein and was waiting for them to catch up.

"Something?" Fargo asked.

"Maybe you can talk a little louder so the Bannocks will hear."

"That's uncalled for," California Jim said.

Badger scowled. "I didn't say anything about Sadie's blathering. She's female. Or about Tom's. He's short on common sense. You two don't have an excuse."

"We're not infants," California Jim said.

"Then stop acting like you are," Badger said, and kneed his mare.

"The gall," California said.

"He's right and you know it."

They pushed on.

Fargo expected the tracks to eventually bring them to the Bannock village. How they would slip in and get the girl and slip out again remained to be seen. They could wait for dark but the Bannocks had dogs and all it would take was a barking mongrel to rouse half the tribe.

Late in the afternoon Badger caught their eye and pointed.

Smoke rose into the sky. Not a lot, but any was a surprise. Indians rarely gave their presence away; they kindled small fires so there was little if any smoke to show where they were.

"Careless of them," California Jim said.

When they could smell the smoke, they stopped and climbed down. The last fifty yards, they crawled.

Fargo came to a log and took off his hat before poking his head up. Below, in a narrow valley, nine young warriors ringed a campfire.

"We're in luck," Badger said. "They stopped early for the night."

"I don't see the girl," California said.

Neither did Fargo.

"You don't reckon they—" California didn't finish.

A tall warrior bent toward the fire to add a piece of tree limb.

"There she is," Fargo said. "Behind the big one."

"Good eyes," Badger said.

"Is that rope around her ankles?" California said. "They must be afraid she'll run off."

"They're too far away for us to pick off from up here," Badger said. "I say we wait until dark, slip on down, and send them to hell."

"Indians have their own hereafter," California Jim said. "They don't go where we do."

"We don't go anywhere," Badger said. "We die and that's it."

"Good God," California said. "You're just like Bear River Tom."

"Have you ever once heard me mention tits?"

Fargo was studying on how best to approach the Bannocks. The forest ended about sixty to seventy feet from the campfire. That was a lot of open space to cover. "Ladies," he said, "save your squabbles for later."

"I don't wear no bonnet," California Jim said indignantly.

They spent what was left of the afternoon watching and waiting.

Sunset was spectacular, painting the sky in vivid hues

of pink and orange and red. The shadows of the trees stretched across the valley floor and over the Bannocks.

The warriors were eating and talking. Now and again the one near the girl glanced at her but the rest paid no attention.

Twilight gave way to night. The Bannock fire was the only glow of light anywhere.

"I reckon it's time," Badger said.

"Why not wait until they turn in?" California Jim suggested.

"I need to be as close as I can when they do." Badger started to rise.

"It should be me," Fargo said.

"Why you? I can be just as sneaky. I've lived with Apaches, the same as you."

"I want it to be me," Fargo said. He couldn't say why. He just did.

"I told you before, I'm the official scout here."

"How about we flip?" California proposed, and slid a coin from his pocket. "Call it."

"Heads," Fargo said.

Heads it was.

Badger didn't like it. "I'll give in this time but don't push me."

Fargo slipped over the rise and down the other side until he was in thick growth. Rising, he glided lower.

Toward the bottom he slowed.

A cluster of boulders was ideal for spying without being seen. He rested his chin on his forearms and listened to the Bannocks banter. Not as versed in their tongue as he was in some others, he caught only a few words he knew.

The warriors weren't disposed to turn in early. Why should they be when they were young and on the warpath, the headiest excitement they could know.

There hadn't been a peep out of Sophie Johnson. But now she sat up and looked at the tall warrior. Her hair was a mess and her dress was streaked with dirt and she looked as sad as a human being could be. "I'm hungry," she said in a small voice.

The warrior acted as if she wasn't there.

"I want something to eat," Sophie said. "Some of that rabbit you cooked."

The warrior still ignored her.

"You promised, Thunder Hawk," Sophie said. "You said I could have something to eat if I behaved."

The remains of the rabbit were on a spit. There wasn't much left, a few strands of meat and bones.

The tall warrior took hold of one end and held it out to her. "Here," he said gruffly.

Sophie snatched it. She was so famished that when she had stripped the meat, she gnawed at the bone. After a bit she said, "There wasn't much of it left. I'm still hungry."

"Stop talk," Thunder Hawk said.

"This is all I get?"

"You lucky get any."

"You're mean. Do you know that?"

"Stop talk or I hit."

"You killed my ma. I saw you with my own eyes. I hate you for that."

"Me kill many whites," Thunder Hawk said.

"I wish you'd killed me," Sophie said. "I want to go home. I want my ma and pa to be alive."

"They dead."

Sophie's eyes filled with tears. "I hate you. I hate you and your people more than anything."

"You Panati now. You learn not hate."

"I'll never be any such thing. I'm a Johnson. I'll always be a Johnson."

"You live with our people. We raise you Panati way."

"I don't want to," Sophie said.

"You do anyway."

"Why didn't you kill me like you did the rest of my family? Why did you bring me with you?"

Thunder Hawk pointed at another warrior. "For Wolf Running. His girl, Morning Flower, die. His wife sad. You be their girl now."

"But you hate whites. I heard you say so."

"Not all whites," Thunder Hawk said. "There one me like. Rest of your kind have bad hearts."

"We do not."

"Whites come to our land. Build what you call fort. Tell us we must do as whites say."

"It's our land now. My pa said so. You're just savages."

Thunder Hawk stared at her. By any standard, he was handsome. He wore his long hair in two braids, and his buckskins were finer than most.

"Quit looking at me like that, consarn you," Sophie Johnson said.

"In ten winters you not hate so much."

"Winters? You mean years?" Sophie asked. "You Indians sure talk strange."

"You learn our tongue. Talk like us."

Sophie made as if to hit him with the rabbit bone. "I'd rather die."

"That so?" Thunder Hawk said, and placed his hand on the knife at his hip.

# 11

Sophie Johnson didn't shrink in fear. She looked Thunder Hawk in the eyes and said, "Go ahead. I dare you. You already killed Ma and Pa and Timmy and Charlie. Kill me too."

They locked stares until Thunder Hawk grunted, and smiled. "You strong. I like that."

"I hate you."

"You not hate always. You grow, you stop. Take time, as your kind say."

"My kind," Sophie repeated. "I'm not your kind and I don't want to be."

"You be daughter to Wolf Running," Thunder Hawk declared. "Make him wife happy again."

"I hate you, hate you, hate you." Sophie sank onto her side with her back to him.

One of the other warriors said something and Thunder Hawk went on at length, apparently translating his conversation. Several of the war party thought it was amusing.

Fargo was more determined than ever to get the girl out of there. He had a long wait ahead.

Starting about ten, the Bannocks began to turn in, one at a time. It was pushing midnight before the second-to-last yawned and stretched and lay down. The last was to stay on watch.

The young warrior added wood to the fire and poked at it with a stick. He shifted. He fidgeted. He kept shaking his head to stay awake.

Fargo stayed flat, awaiting the right moment, as a mountain lion would when stalking deer.

He thought of Jed Crow and Tennessee. It was ironic that they were brought to Fort Carlson by a practical joke, only to meet their end.

Scouting wasn't for the timid. Or for the careless. All it took was a moment's distraction, and death came swift and sure. The scouts who lasted the longest were those who learned their lesson from the deer. They never let down their guard. They never gave life the chance to bury its fangs in their neck.

Fargo rarely let down his. He lived on the razor's edge, and liked it.

The young warrior did more fidgeting. He got up and walked in a circle around the sleepers. He checked the horses. He stared at the stars. He gazed into the night to the south, east, west, and north. He sat back down and added more wood and the fire flared brighter than older warriors would let it.

Fargo didn't like that. The smaller the fire, the less light, the easier for him. Now the ring of light was twice what it had been. He'd have to be lightning quick to get in, get the girl, and get out again.

Presently the young warrior's chin bobbed. He fought it. He jerked his head up and blinked and stretched. Then his head bobbed again and he went through the same thing.

The intervals between each bob became shorter and shorter until finally his chin sank and didn't rise. He had fallen asleep.

The moment had come.

Fargo crawled. He forced himself to go slow so the grass wouldn't rustle. Holding his head high enough to see the Bannocks, he was halfway to the fire when the young warrior jerked and sat upright.

Fargo froze.

The warrior sheepishly looked at the sleepers and then anxiously stared all around, and relaxed. The fire had burned down a little and he groped the ground but he had used the last of the firewood. He stared at the trees.

Uh-oh, Fargo thought. He was directly between the fire

and more firewood. He hoped the young warrior would wait a while before coming for more, but no such luck.

The Bannock stood. Bending, he selected a burning brand, raised it over his head, and came toward the woods.

Fargo tried to sink into the earth.

The young man glanced right and left. He was nervous. Fargo wondered if the warrior sensed him but then decided that no, it was the night. The youngster was scared of the dark.

Some whites thought that was a white trait, that because Indians lived in the wild, they were used to the dark and went about without fear. But Indians knew that night was when the meat-eaters filled their bellies. Some tribes, too, believed that night was when other things were abroad, things they feared even more than grizzlies and mountains lions, things their forefathers feared, horrific things from the dawn of time. To say nothing of the many tribes that believed in ghosts.

So the young Bannock's fear, while it might seem childish, was understandable. He advanced slowly, moving the torch back and forth, his other hand on his knife.

Fargo was willing to let the Bannock go past and then go for the girl. But the warrior was coming right at him. Quickly, Fargo holstered his Colt. Sliding his leg toward his chest, he slipped his hand under his pant leg and into his boot and palmed the Arkansas toothpick.

The young warrior was taking his sweet time. Every few strides he stopped to look around.

Fargo checked on the others at the fire. None had stirred.

The light from the burning brand was about to wash over him.

Then a shooting star blazed the heavens and the young warrior craned his head to watch it streak across the sky. The Bannocks took shooting stars to be omens.

So did Fargo. He was up and reached him in a rush. He thought of the slain mother and the dead boys as he rammed his toothpick to the hilt just below the Bannock's sternum.

The young warrior never so much as opened his mouth to cry out. He died on his feet, and Fargo lowered him and yanked the toothpick out.

The other warriors had gone on sleeping.

A horse raised its head and pricked its ears but didn't whinny or stomp.

Fargo wiped the toothpick on the dead warrior's leggings, crouched, and crept closer. The slightest sound could give him away. He stopped each time a Bannock moved. When one of them muttered, he stopped dead, thinking the warrior was about to sit up.

Sophie Johnson was curled into a ball, her head tucked to her chest and her arms wrapped around herself, as if she was trying to climb into her own body.

Fargo switched the toothpick to his left hand so his right was free to draw the Colt if he had to.

Now two of the horses were staring at him. Neither acted agitated, but all it would take was a nicker.

Suddenly, a little ways up the valley, a coyote yipped. A normal enough sound; coyotes did that often at night. But a warrior gave a snort and sleepily rose onto an elbow.

Fargo froze again. He was in clear sight if the man should turn his head.

The warrior scratched himself, and sluggishly yawned.

Conveniently, the coyote chose that moment to yip once more.

With a grunt, the warrior sank back down, his cheek cradled on his arm.

Fargo didn't move a muscle until he was sure the man was asleep. Low to the ground, he snuck around to Sophie Johnson.

Thunder Hawk was only five feet away, on his side, snoring lightly.

Fargo started to reach for the girl, and hesitated. If she woke with a start, as she might well do given the circumstances, she was liable to shout and wake the war party.

Sliding the toothpick into its sheath, Fargo took a gamble. He placed his hand over her mouth, put his mouth to her ear, and whispered, "Sophie, I'm a friend. I'm here to help you get away."

Her eyes flew open and her whole body stiffened.

"I'm a friend," Fargo whispered again. "Don't make a sound or we're in trouble."

The whites of her eyes were showing. She was frightened, but to her credit she stayed calm.

"I'm going to untie you," Fargo whispered, "and we'll get out of here."

Hope lit her face.

Fargo moved his hand from her mouth and bent over her ankles. He pried at the knots but they resisted his efforts to loosen them. Frustrated, he resorted to the toothpick. A couple of slashes, and the girl's legs were free. He replaced the knife.

Sophie watched his every movement as if her life depended on it—which it did.

Putting a finger to his lips to caution her to stay quiet, Fargo looped his arm around her waist and hoisted her off the ground. She wrapped her arms around his neck and clung fast.

None of the Bannocks stirred.

Fargo started to circle back the way he had come.

Sophie stared at the warriors and quaked and pressed her face to his neck. She was afraid one would wake up.

Fargo forced himself to go slow even though his every instinct was to bolt, to run for it and trust to the night to conceal them and the forest to keep them safe once they were under cover.

All the horses were watching.

Something in the fire crackled and popped, and there was a hiss.

The same warrior who had woken up when the coyote yipped, woke up again. He raised his head and gazed at the fire and rolled over and went back to sleep.

Every nerve taut, Fargo let half a minute go by before

he took his next step. He was almost past the still forms when he was taken aback by Sophie unexpectedly raising her head to whisper in his ear.

"Who are you?"

"Not now."

"I want to know your name. I never saw you before. How do I know I can trust you?"

"The Bannocks," Fargo whispered, thinking that should be enough.

"I want to know your name, mister," she insisted with the typical stubbornness of a child her age.

"Skye Fargo."

"Your folks named you after the sky? I know a girl who was named after a daisy."

"You really need to be quiet," Fargo urged. He had half a mind to clamp his hand over her mouth but she might struggle.

"How did you know they took me? Was it my pa who sent you?"

"Quiet, damn it, girl."

Sophie gasped.

Fargo wanted to kick himself. He'd forgotten she was only ten. "We can talk when it's safe," he said, and took another step.

That was when the warrior who had already woken up twice woke up a third time—and stood.

# 12

Fargo stayed perfectly still. Sophie Johnson tensed and dug her nails in deep but didn't utter a peep.

This time it didn't matter. This time the warrior turned, and saw them.

Several seconds went by. The Bannock stared and Fargo stared and Sophie tried to crawl into his neck.

And then came the inevitable—the warrior opened his mouth to shout.

Fargo drew the Colt and fired. The slug smashed the warrior off his feet and brought the others scrambling up off the ground.

Sophie bleated in fright, and Fargo ran. He had no hankering to fight the whole war party.

A warrior spotted him right away and pointed and shouted.

Sophie Johnson whimpered.

Fargo glanced back. Two warriors hadn't bothered grabbing bows; they'd drawn knives and were bounding in pursuit. He churned his legs, thinking if he could reach cover he could elude them. But God, they were fast. Faster than he was. He was almost to the woods when the first was on top of him.

Fargo thrust out the Colt and fired without stopping. The lead cored the warrior's chest, killing him outright. But momentum carried the body forward, and into Fargo. He felt the other's leg entangle with his.

Sophie shrieked as they went down.

Fargo landed on his shoulder so he bore the brunt. The body was on top of him and he shoved it off with the same hand that held the Colt, just as the second fleet-footed warrior reached him and raised a knife to stab.

Fargo shot him in the head. He didn't watch the husk collapse. He was up and running again, Sophie clutched tight. An arrow whizzed past his neck. Another missed his arm by a cat's whisker.

The trees closed around them and Fargo swerved to avoid colliding with one.

High above them rifles boomed.

Emmett Badger and California Jim were covering his escape.

Fargo flew. Behind him the undergrowth crackled and he realized at least one of the Bannocks had also made it to the trees. He swerved right, ran straight for a short distance, then swerved to the right again and stopped in his tracks and squatted.

The crackling and snapping was close. It, too, stopped, and Fargo knew the warrior was straining his ears to catch some sound of them.

"Why did you stop?" Sophie whispered.

Fargo was up before she stopped asking. He was sure the warrior had heard her and the pounding of moccasin-shod feet proved him right. He zigged. He zagged. He raced around a thicket. He barely spotted a log in time to vault over it. He was in midleap when inspiration struck, and when his boots thudded down, he spun and flung himself behind the log and pressed Sophie against it.

"Don't move!" Fargo whispered in his best you'd-better-listen-or-else voice. He was still holding the Colt, and he cocked it just as a figure leaped over the log, and over them.

Fargo figured to shoot as the warrior landed. But the Bannock must have seen him drop behind the log and did an incredible thing. In the middle of his leap, the warrior twisted around and came down on both feet inches from where they lay. Fargo extended the Colt at the same instant the warrior slashed with a tomahawk. Metal met metal and the Colt went flying.

Letting go of Sophie, Fargo pushed up. The tomahawk

arced at his face and he grabbed the warrior's wrist in both hands, and wrenched. He thought he could force the Bannock to drop it but the young warrior clung tenaciously and drove a knee at his gut.

It felt as if Fargo's stomach smashed against his spine. Involuntarily, he doubled over. The warrior sought to wrest his arm free, and drove the same knee at Fargo's nose. Fargo got a forearm between them, absorbing most of the blow. Most, but not all. His head rocked and it was a wonder his nose didn't break. He tottered, and the Bannock dug iron fingers into his throat. His boots bumped something that moved.

Sophie Johnson screamed.

Fargo's left foot hooked the log. He lost his balance and gravity took over. He wound up with the warrior on top of him, trying to choke him while simultaneously seeking to use that tomahawk to deadly effect.

Fargo couldn't breathe. His vision swam. In desperation he smashed his forehead into the warrior's face. There was a crunch, and wet drops spattered his cheeks. The Bannock howled in rage more than pain and drew back.

Somehow Fargo found his boot. The Arkansas toothpick was where it should be, and he buried it in the other man's ribs. The Bannock cried out and tried to pull away, and Fargo rammed the cold steel up in under the warrior's jaw. More wet drops rained, and suddenly deadweight was on his chest.

Fargo lay still, catching his breath, his blood roaring in his ears.

"Mister?" Sophie whispered.

Fargo swallowed but couldn't find his voice. It had been *that* close.

"Mister? Are you dead?"

"Not yet," Fargo whispered. He almost added, "No thanks to you." He pushed at the body but it refused to budge.

"You scared me," Sophie said. "I thought you were a goner."

Fargo pushed harder. The body still wouldn't move, and he swore.

"My ma says you shouldn't ought to talk like that," Sophie said. "When pa does, she makes him say he's sorry."

"I'm not sorry," Fargo said, and heaved. The lifeless lump rolled to one side and he managed to rise high enough to sit on the log.

"You must be a foul mouth," Sophie said.

"A what?" Fargo realized the shooting had stopped. Either the Bannocks had fled or they had reached the forest, and cover.

"That's what Ma calls people who use words like you do," Sophie enlightened him. "Foulmouthed."

Fargo thought he heard the crunch of a twig. Sliding off the log, he put his hand over the girl's mouth. "Quiet. There are more Indians."

For once she shut up.

Lifting her, Fargo crept away. The climb grew steep, the undergrowth thick. In order to avoid making noise, he had to go slower than a tortoise.

It was taking so long that Sophie squirmed and finally whispered, "Where's your horse? You did bring one, didn't you? You're not going to carry me all the way?"

"Do you want my hand over your mouth again?"

"No," she said. "It smells funny."

Fargo didn't know what to make of that. He sniffed his other palm. It smelled fine to him.

They were skirting a spruce when a figure materialized, in front of them, not behind them.

Fargo was looking behind them and wouldn't have noticed except that Sophie bleated in alarm.

"An Injun!"

Fargo spun and brought up the Colt.

"Are you or her hurt?"

"Badger?" Fargo said. He was impressed at how silently the other scout moved. In more ways than one, the man was every bit his equal.

"It's my voice, isn't it?" Badger said.

Another figure appeared.

"We think one of the Bannocks made it into the trees after you, pard," California Jim said.

"He's been taken care of."

"The sky man stabbed him," Sophie said proudly. "Killed him dead."

"The rest skedaddled," California revealed, "so you're safe enough."

"For now," Badger said.

California grinned at Sophie and held out an arm. "Want me to carry the sprout for a spell?"

"No," Sophie said, and pressed against Fargo. "I want you to carry me."

"It's true what they say," Badger quipped. "You sure have a way with the ladies."

California snickered.

"Why is that funny?" Sophie asked.

"Pay them no mind," Fargo said. "They're both touched in the head."

"They should be in a what do you call it?" Sophie said.

"Call what?"

"Now I remember. Ma called it an asylum. Her aunt had a fall and hurt her head, and she went around making cat sounds. Ma said she was touched in the head, and they put her in an asylum. We went to visit her once. It was awful. She meowed and licked herself. There was a man who kept sniffing everybody and growling. And another man who said he liked to dance with snakes. And another who—"

"The Bannocks might come back," Badger said.

"Tell me about the asylum later," Fargo suggested to the girl. "We have to light a shuck."

"Shouldn't we take them there?" Sophie asked.

"Take who where?"

"These two," Sophie said, with a nod at California Jim and Badger. "You said they should be in an asylum."

California snickered anew.

"He does that a lot," Sophie said.

"Are we going to stand here listening to her babble all night?" Badger asked.

"Hey," Sophie said.

Fargo headed up the mountain. Once over the crest

they descended to the horses. He swung Sophie over the saddle and was about to climb up when she bent toward him to whisper.

"I have to go."

"We're going now," Fargo said.

"No, I have to *go*."

"As soon as I'm on, we're leaving."

"No," Sophie said, sounding annoyed. "I have to wee-wee."

"Wee-wee?" Fargo said.

"Ma said to never say the other word. But those Injuns had me tied up an awful long while and the mean one said they wouldn't let me go until the sun came up."

"She has to pee," Badger said.

"I know that," Fargo said testily.

California snickered.

Fargo swung her down and patted her on the back. "Off you go."

"In the dark?"

"You just said you had to."

"Alone? You have to come with me."

"Like hell."

California let out a full-bellied laugh. "You have to excuse my pard, little lady. He's never had kids of his own. Want me to take you?"

"No. I don't know you. I want him." Sophie clasped Fargo's hand. "Or don't you care if a bear eats me?"

"True love," Badger said.

Fargo sighed and said something he never in his life thought he would say. "I'll take you to wee-wee."

# 13

They rode all night but it wasn't until near noon of the next day that their mounts came to a weary stop at a hitch rail on Salt Creek's dusty main street. No sooner did they draw rein than people came from everywhere.

Sagebrush Sadie and Bear River Tom were part of an exodus from the saloon. Tom clapped Fargo on the back and exclaimed, "You got her, pup!"

A fuss was made. The settlers gushed with thanks.

A young couple, friends of the Johnson family, offered to take Sophie off Fargo's hands.

"But I want to stay with him," the girl said, clinging to his neck.

"That wouldn't do," the woman said. "Horace and me have talked it over and we're willing to take you in if we can't find kin who claim you."

Sophie shook her head and pressed her cheek to Fargo's. "But he saved me."

"You could marry him," Badger said.

California Jim did more of his infernal snickering.

Sophie looked at them and at Fargo and at the woman and said, "Can I? Can I marry him, Matilda?"

"Oh, hell," Fargo said.

Sophie pulled back and regarded him as if he had bit her. "I forgot you're a foul mouth. Ma said never to have anything to do with foul mouths."

"Your mother was a smart woman," Matilda said. "You should do as she told you."

"I'm sorry," Sophie said to Fargo. "I reckon I can't marry you, after all."

"Dang," Badger said.

And that was that. Relieved, and tired to his marrow, Fargo shouldered out of the press of the grateful and through the batwings. He needed sleep but he also needed a drink. He wasn't alone long.

"That was awful decent, what you did," Sagebrush Sadie said at his elbow.

"You'd have done the same."

Sadie leaned on the bar. "Tom and me didn't bury Tennessee. We figured you and the others would want to be there for the planting. We have the body wrapped in a blanket over in a root cellar. The townspeople offered to keep it for us until you got back."

The last thing Fargo wanted to do was attend a funeral. But he said, "Great folks hereabouts," and took a grateful swig.

"You sound bitter."

"They shouldn't be here."

"Who?"

"These idiots," Fargo said, with a sweep of his arm that encompassed the saloon and the settlement. "Building a settlement in the middle of Bannock country. And the Johnsons, homesteading where they did."

"People never let a lack of brains stop them from living," Sadie said.

"It sure as hell doesn't stop them from dying."

"I still can't rightly blame them," Sadie said. "I've done my own share of stupid things."

From outside came a loud laugh. Bear River Tom thought something was hilarious.

"I wish it had been you here with me and not him," Sadie remarked.

"He got frisky?"

"He knows better," Sadie said. "I'd shoot him as soon as look at him if he so much as touched me. It's just that he never shuts up. And the one thing he likes to talk about most is—" She stopped.

"Tits," Fargo said.

Sadie nodded. "I swear, that man has tits for brains. His ma must have suckled him until he was twelve."

Fargo did some laughing of his own.

"Anyway," Sadie said. "What now? We still have no idea who brought us here, or why, and I'd sure like to find out."

"You and me, both." Fargo wasn't the least little bit amused by the letters, especially now that they had cost the lives of Jed Crow and Tennessee.

"Speaking of which," Sadie said, "how about we take this bottle and go off into the woods and be by ourselves for a spell?"

Fargo looked at her. Coming out of the blue, as it did, her invite puzzled him. "What happens if *I* get frisky?" He was only half joking. She had a body that any hot-blooded male would love to get his hands on.

Sagebrush Sadie looked him in the eyes and said, "I wouldn't shoot you like I'd shoot Bear River Tom."

Fargo was of two minds. Part of him, the sensible part, craved rest. He had been up for more than twenty-four hours, riding and fighting hard, and needed sleep. But the other part of him, the part that perked at a pretty face and twitched at shapely legs, perked up now.

Sadie must have misconstrued his hesitation. "Why wouldn't I want to? So what if I wear britches instead of a dress? I have needs the same as any gal."

"I didn't know you were interested."

Sadie surprised him by saying something he had said to women a hundred times or more. "Don't make more of it than there is. It's not like I want to be man and wife."

"You're an independent lady," Fargo said by way of a compliment, and was surprised when she bristled.

"What's that supposed to mean? A woman can't do man's work? I've been hearing that all my life."

"Hell, Sadie," Fargo said. "I only meant you stand on your own two feet."

"You're damn right I do. And I'll go on being as I like to be until the day I die."

"Good for you."

Sadie didn't seem to hear him. "I am sick to death of people who won't accept me as I am. Of always having to prove myself because I'm female. I can do anything you or California or Tom can do but everyone thinks I can't just because I'm a woman."

"Not everyone," Fargo said. "We know how good you are."

Sadie blushed slightly. "Thank you. I'm sorry about the outburst. It's the rest of the world that judges a person by whether they have a peter or not."

"I have one," Fargo said, and gave the junction of her thighs a pointed look.

"Oh my," Sadie said. She grinned and leaned toward him. "We'll sneak off and not tell the others where we're going. It's none of their damn business, anyhow, and I'd rather not be teased."

Fargo deemed that reasonable. "They'll see us as soon as we walk out."

Sadie pondered a few moments. "You slip out the back, and I'll fetch my horse and yours. If anyone asks, I'll say I'm bedding him down for you. Then I come get you and off we go."

It seemed a little silly to go to such lengths but Fargo didn't want to spoil her mood so he nodded.

"We can be back by nightfall with no one the wiser." Sadie smiled and hurried out.

Fargo drained his glass and strolled out the back to wait. It wasn't long before hooves clattered and around the saloon rode Sadie, leading the Ovaro by the reins.

"Here you go. Everyone is still fussing over that girl and no one noticed."

Swinging up, Fargo asked, "Do you have a particular spot in mind?"

"As a matter of fact, I do." Sadie grinned and moved past him, up the valley toward Fort Carlson.

Fargo couldn't imagine why she'd want to go there.

It wasn't long, though, before Sadie turned up a gully that knifed a slope and wound up its serpentine length to a bench that afforded a spectacular view of Salt Valley.

She didn't stop there. She continued into the forest to a pine-hemmed hummock aglow in brilliant shafts of mote-filled sunbeams.

Drawing rein, she gazed happily around. "What do you think?"

"Pretty," Fargo said, but he was thinking something else.

"We'll have it all to ourselves. No one ever comes here." Sadie swung her leg over her saddle horn and slid off. "Don't sit up there all day."

Fargo climbed down and pressed a hand to the small of his back. "How did you know this spot was here?"

"I beg your pardon?"

"A person could ride right by it and not know."

"Oh." Sadie smiled sweetly. "This isn't the first time I've been to the Salt Range. I get around a lot, just like you do, I'd imagine." She motioned. "How about we get a fire going? I'll gather up the firewood."

Fargo would rather get right to the reason they were there, but if the lady wanted a fire, it was fine by him. Opening his saddlebags, he took out his lucifers.

Sadie wasn't gone long. She returned with an armful of broken limbs and sticks. "I found this for kindling," she said, and showed him an old bird's nest.

Fargo did the honors. The nest ignited at the touch of a lucifer. He made a teepee of sticks and when small flames crawled up them, he added a few branches and soon had a fire crackling.

Sadie opened her own saddlebags and came over holding something behind her back. "Guess what I brought."

"Monongahela?"

Sadie held out a bottle. "I always have one handy for snake bites and such."

"A gal after my own heart," Fargo said. Taking it, he treated himself to a long swill. "Always hits the spot," he said, and smacked his lips.

"I reckoned it would help us relax and make the most of, you know."

Fargo didn't point out that when it came to *that*, he

77

made the most of it without needing liquor. A woman's naked body was intoxicating enough.

"It sure helps me," Sadie said. Accepting the bottle, she swallowed, and coughed. "Believe it or not, I don't drink all that much except when I make love."

Fargo couldn't say the same.

"I don't handle liquor all that well," Sadie prattled on. "It makes me sick as a dog."

"Go easy on the coffin varnish, then," Fargo advised. He wouldn't like to have come all that way for nothing.

"Oh, don't worry. I'm not letting anything spoil this." Sadie chuckled. "I've looked forward to cavorting with you since we met."

"You could have fooled me." Fargo usually knew when a woman was interested. There were telltale signs, none of which Sadie had exhibited.

"I did it to fool the others," Sadie said. "Who I let touch me is none of their damn business."

"Speaking of touching," Fargo said.

Sadie put a hand to his chest. "Hold your horses. I need to work up to it. I'm shy, believe it or not."

"Take however long you need," Fargo generously offered. It was a small sacrifice to make for the privilege of poking her.

"You're awful considerate."

Fargo added another stick to the fire while admiring the swell of her bosom and those delectable full lips.

Sadie noticed, and grinned. Setting down the bottle, she showed that she wasn't quite as shy as she claimed; she cupped her breasts and said huskily, "See anything you like?"

# 14

Fargo didn't know what to make of her. He tried to recollect if he'd ever heard tell of her giving someone a tumble in the hay, and couldn't. For all he knew, she was as pure as the driven snow. And now this.

"What are you waiting for?" Sagebrush Sadie asked with a come-and-touch-me smile.

"Are we in a hurry and I didn't know it?"

Sadie lowered her hands. "No. I just reckoned"—she stopped, and gestured—"I'm trying to excite you. Guess I'm not much good at it."

By rights, Fargo should be excited as hell. But something was nagging at him. He couldn't figure what, and that annoyed him.

"The stories they tell about you," Sadie said with a smile, "I naturally figured you'd have ripped my clothes off by now."

"I've heard the same stories." Fargo took the bottle and chugged. The whiskey would loosen him up. And give him time to think. His uncharacteristic hesitation made no sense. It took a lot to blunt his desire. The deaths of Jed Crow and Tennessee weren't enough; he hadn't known either all that well. If it had been California Jim or even Bear River Tom, it would be different.

"Are you fixing to sit there all damn day?" Sadie said, sounding irritated.

"Don't plan on it," Fargo said, and indulged in another swallow.

"The great cocksman Skye Fargo," Sadie said sarcastically. "To get you to perform, I guess a gal has to wrestle you out of your britches."

"I'm not a trained bear," Fargo growled.

"Is that how I'm treating you? I'm sorry. I told you I don't do this a lot." Sadie folded her hands in her lap. "Whenever you're ready is fine by me."

Fargo looked at her mouth and the twin bulges on her chest and admired how wonderfully long her legs were, and wanted to hit himself with the whiskey bottle. What in hell was he waiting for? Setting it down, he slid closer.

She sat still as he put an arm around her shoulders, cupped her chin, and kissed her on the mouth. She still just sat there. Thinking he might have spoiled her mood, he kissed her again, rimming her lips with his tongue even as he molded her back as if it were clay.

Gradually, he felt her relax. He kissed a cheek and an ear and nipped her lobe. When he licked her neck, she shivered. He sucked on her throat and bit her chin.

A hunger came into her eyes. "That's more like it," she said softly.

"You're not one of those females who likes to jabber while she does it?" Fargo asked.

"My lips are sealed."

"I hope not." Fargo pressed his to hers and the kiss went on a long time, with her squirming and cooing like a dove.

This was more like it. Fargo stirred, his bulge growing when he covered a breast. He could feel her nipple, rigid as a tack, through her buckskin shirt. He squeezed and pinched and she groaned and lavished tiny kisses on his throat.

Fargo eased her down so she was flat on her back. Stretching out beside her, he undid her gun belt. She glanced down as if she didn't like him doing that, but how else were they to do the deed? He sought to relax her even more by kissing and fondling and caressing her longer than he normally would. He wanted her ripe and ready, and to enjoy it as much as he did. Women sometimes went for a second helping if the first was to their taste.

He got her shirt up over her breasts; they were glorious, full and round and sensitive to his slightest touch. When he inhaled a nipple and sucked, she closed her eyes and moaned and dug her fingernails into his shoulders.

He switched to her other breast and gave it the same lathering.

Beside them the fire popped. Both horses were dozing. The woods were quiet and still.

Sadie unfastened his belt and slid his shirt up his chest. "Oh, my," she whispered when she saw his corded muscles. "You have a dandy body. I could eat you alive."

"Be my guest."

She grinned, and kissed his chest and his ribs and his washboard belly. She stuck the tip of her tongue in his navel and swirled it.

By then Fargo had a redwood between his legs. He started to slide her pants down and she stiffened slightly.

She wasn't quite primed.

Fargo was nothing if not patient. He went on stroking her. Sliding a hand to her left knee, he brought it up to her inner thighs, rubbing in small circles.

She was hot down there, almost as hot as the fire. He ran a finger between her legs and she clutched him and gasped.

When he cupped her nether mount, her eyes widened and she looked at him with a strange fierce intensity. He had a sense that she had been telling the truth about not being very experienced.

This time she didn't tense when he commenced to slide her pants down. He had to remove her boots to get them all the way off.

At last she was naked. He took a few moments to drink in the sight—her sun-bronzed, beautiful face, the paler skin the sun seldom touched, the twin slopes of her melons, her thatch lower down, and the velvet sweep of those winsome legs.

"Like what you see, big man?" Sadie husked, and damned if she didn't blush.

"Like it a lot," Fargo said. Their mouths locked and he

set to caressing every square inch of her that he could reach.

Off in the woods a finch chirped. Otherwise the woodland was undisturbed.

Fargo parted her nether lips and Sadie tried to suck his tongue into her throat. He rubbed, and she ground her hips into his. When his finger penetrated her, she threw back her head and for a second he thought she would cry out, but she bit her lip and trembled. He inserted a second finger, and pumped, and she tried to thrust herself into his palm.

She was wet. She was eager. She was as ready as she would ever be.

Easing onto his knees between her legs, Fargo touched the tip of his pole to her sheath. She looked him in the eyes with that same fierce intensity, and gave a nod of her chin.

Slow or hard, that was the question. Fargo chose hard. He rammed up into her. Now she did cry out, and raked his arms with her nails. She kissed him almost savagely.

Cupping her bottom, Fargo rocked her to the heights of carnal release. She mewed. She clawed. She was a she-cat, unleashed. In her ardor she drew blood but that was all right. A little pain added spice to pleasure.

They burned a slow fuse to their explosion.

Fargo held off as long as he could. She went over the brink first, thrashing and crying, "Oh! Oh! Oh!"

Then came his turn, and it was as it always was: better than whiskey, better than food, better than cards, better than anything, ever.

If someone were to ask him what he liked most in this world, he'd say wandering where the wind took him—and this.

Afterward, they lay side by side, breathing heavily, the sweat slowly cooling on their overheated bodies.

Sadie's eyes were closed, and he thought she had drifted asleep until she quietly said, "I'd wondered how it was."

"What?" he sluggishly asked.

"You. The stories they tell."

"Don't believe everything you hear."

"This time they were right. They say you're a stallion, and you are."

"Keep it to yourself," Fargo said, "but the Ovaro and me are brothers."

Sadie laughed. "Thank you for doing me. I liked it a lot."

"Hell," Fargo said sleepily. He wouldn't mind drifting off. He was so damn tried.

"You've had Indian ladies, too, I hear," Sadie mentioned.

Yes, Fargo had. More than a few. He smiled at the memories.

"It's good you're not like so many other whites."

Fargo wished she would shut up and let him sleep. He didn't answer, thinking she would take the hint.

"Those who think the only good redskin is one who isn't breathing. Me, I've lived with one of the tribes. They're people, just like you and me."

Fargo agreed.

"I can't stand it that people hate other people over the color of their skin, when under that skin, they're more alike than they are willing to admit."

"You're preaching to the choir," Fargo said.

Sadie wouldn't let it drop. "You make a friend of an Indian and you have a friend for life."

"I could use some sleep," Fargo bluntly brought up.

"Oh. Sorry."

Fargo settled back. He was almost under when he became aware of sounds, and movement, and he reluctantly cracked an eyelid.

Sadie was dressing.

Fargo was surprised. Most women liked a nap after.

He opened both eyes.

Sadie had pulled her britches on and reached for her shirt. She was about to slide it over her head when she glanced at him and gave a start. "I thought you'd fallen asleep."

"No such luck." Fargo sighed and sat up.

"You don't have to get up on my account. Sleep as long as you'd like."

"You're not sleeping."

"I'm not tired," Sadie said. "Lie back down. I'll keep watch and wake you in an hour or so."

Fargo began to put himself together.

"Didn't you hear me?" Sadie sounded upset that she had spoiled his nap.

"I'm not tired, either," Fargo lied.

Sadie frowned. "I'll feel bad if you don't. Please. I insist."

"Enough," Fargo said grumpily. She was making too much of a fuss. He'd take her to the settlement and go off by himself to get some sleep.

"Tell you what. I'll get my blanket and you can use it as a pillow."

Fargo was about to tell her he didn't want a pillow, that he was perfectly fine, and would be even finer if she would shut the hell up.

Then the Ovaro raised its head, pricked its ears, and whinnied.

# 15

Fargo straightened and put his hand on his holster, which was on the ground next to him.

"What's the matter?" Sadie asked.

Nodding at the Ovaro, Fargo rose to his knees, pulled his shirt down, and quickly strapped his gun belt around his waist.

"It could be anything," Sadie said. "Maybe it caught the scent of a bear or a wolf."

"Or Bannocks."

"There aren't any within twenty miles," Sadie said. "I'd stake my hide on it."

"Stake yours all you want." Fargo wasn't about to stake his. Rising, he adjusted his hat and went to the stallion. It was still staring into the trees. He looked in the same direction but saw no cause for alarm.

"Anything?" Sadie asked. She was on her feet, her rifle in her hands.

Fargo shook his head.

"See?" Sadie laughed. "I told you it was nothing to worry about."

An arrow whisked out of the forest and missed the Ovaro's neck by a hand's-width. Simultaneously, several piercing war whoops shattered the stillness on both sides of the hummock.

Before they faded, Fargo was in the saddle and had reined around and slicked the Colt out. He glimpsed a swarthy figure notching an arrow and banged off two shots.

Sagebrush Sadie was glued in place, staring at him with her mouth agape.

"What the hell are you waiting for?" Fargo roared. He fired at a moving shape, saw that Sadie still hadn't moved, and, bending, grabbed the reins to her animal and pulled the horse toward her.

Sadie just stood there.

"Get on your damn horse," Fargo bellowed. He twisted, spotted several fast-moving silhouettes, and fired to discourage them.

Sadie *still* hadn't budged.

Fargo kicked her. He unhooked his boot from the stirrup and drove the toe into her shoulder. "Get on your goddamn horse *now*."

Sadie blinked, and came out of herself. Nodding, she sprang to her saddle and was up and on in a twinkling. "Sorry," she blurted.

So far Fargo had spied warriors to the north and the south. He reined to the east and was about to use his spurs when a shaft streaked out the pines and flew past his head.

That left west. Again Fargo hauled on the reins. Again he was confronted by moving silhouettes. To hell with it, he thought. At a gallop he charged into the woods. An arrow flashed in front of his face. A bare-chested warrior came at him with a lance poised, and he cored the Bannock's brain. He swept around several spruce, hugging the saddle, and rode for dear life.

A glance showed that Sadie was right behind him, her mouth set in a grim line.

Angry cries replaced the war whoops. Warriors rushed to head them off but fortunately they'd left their own horses off in the trees.

Fargo didn't stop until he had put a good half mile behind him. There was no evidence of pursuit. Pushing his hat back, he ran a hand across his brow. "That was a close one."

Sadie glumly nodded. "I'm afraid I forgot the whiskey bottle."

Fargo studied her. "What got into you back there? You acted like a damn greenhorn."

"I froze."

"Do that again and you'll be keeping Jed Crow and Tennessee company."

"It hasn't ever happened before."

"And it better not again," Fargo cautioned.

"It must have been our lovemaking," Sadie said. "I wasn't myself. I felt so good there for a little bit, I almost forgot."

"Forgot what?"

"Where I was."

Fargo let it drop. They were alive and in one piece, and that was what counted. He pointed the Ovaro toward the settlement.

Sadie hung back. She seemed troubled by their narrow escape.

The afternoon waned and twilight fell. A smattering of lights blossomed in Salt Creek, more as the sky blackened.

Sadie caught up to him. "I want to apologize again for how I behaved."

"No need."

"You were right. I make a habit of freezing up, I won't be around long."

"What I don't savvy," Fargo said, giving voice to something he had been mulling, "is how they found us."

"This is Bannock territory," Sadie said, implying that were explanation enough.

"A territory that covers hundreds of square miles," Fargo brought up. "And we didn't see any sign of them on our way there."

Sadie shrugged. "A war party came across our sign and stalked us. Happens all the time."

Fargo supposed so. But it still bothered him. This made three times the Bannocks had jumped them. Once or twice he could chalk up to coincidence, but three?

"You think on things too much," Sadie said.

"How about we stop and I do you again?"

"Here and now?"

"One spot of grass is as good as another."

Sadie laughed. "Goodness, you're a randy goat. But, no, thank you. Once was enough."

"I must be losing my touch," Fargo said.

"Not hardly."

Salt Creek's nightlife was in full swing, such as it was. The saloon was half-full with settlers drinking and playing cards.

A plump dove with quite possibly the largest breasts on the planet moved among them, touching and smiling and encouraging them to drink.

The first thing Fargo did was buy a bottle. The second was to amble over to a table where California Jim was in a card game. "How's your luck?"

"Pard!" California exclaimed in surprise. "I was wondering where you got to." He tapped his cards. "I'm having a good run. I won ten cents the last hand and five cents a few hands before that."

"Cents?" Fargo said.

"Twenty-cent limit," a burly local in a derby said. "We ain't rich hereabouts."

Several others nodded.

"Hell," Fargo said. He gazed around. "Where did Bear River Tom and Badger get to?"

"Badger had to report to the fort," California replied. "The colonel sent for him. As for Tom, he fell in love with that lady with the big tits. Lily, her name is. He paid for a poke and they went off and she came back but he didn't." California's turn to bet came and he raised five cents. "Are you fixing to sit in and win a fortune?"

"Maybe some other life," Fargo said. He spied an empty table in a corner and went over before someone claimed it. Hooking a chair with his boot, he sat with his back to the wall and commenced to drink in earnest. He wasn't hankering for company but he got some anyway. A cloud of perfume fit to gag a mule wreathed him, and he was eye to eye with Lily's enormous jugs.

"What do we have here?" she asked throatily.

"I already had some today," Fargo said, "but thank you for the offer."

Lily laughed. "Why, listen to you. And I've had some, too."

"With Bear River Tom," Fargo said. "I heard."

"He's a strange one," Lily said. "All he cared about were my tits. He made love to them and not the rest of me."

Fargo's whiskey went down the wrong pipe, and he sputtered. "He did what?"

"You heard me," Lily said. "I couldn't get him to touch my legs or anything else. For him it was tits and only tits."

"Where is Mr. Tit now?"

"Beats me. After we were done, he lay there muttering to himself. About the Bannocks, of all things. Then he got up and went off, saying there was something he had to do."

Lily came closer and placed a pudgy hand on his arm. "Nice broad shoulders you have."

"I thank you again, but no."

Lily rimmed her ruby lips with the pink tip of her tongue. "You can't blame a gal for trying. You're awful easy on the eyes. If you change your mind, look me and my tits up."

"If I do, I will."

Lily touched his ear, winked, and sashayed away, her rump reminding him of the broad side of a barn.

"What are you grinning at?" Sagebrush Sadie asked, claiming a chair across from him.

"Stables and such."

Sadie crooked an eyebrow but didn't ask him to explain. She had a beer and took a swallow, leaving a foam mustache on her upper lip. "I just talked to California Jim. He says he's planning to stay here tonight. How about you?"

"I haven't made up my mind yet."

"I was thinking of going to the fort," Sadie said. "Word is the army is fixing to take steps to contain the renegades."

"Contain?" Fargo said.

"That's what the barkeep told me. And he got it straight

from a soldier's mouth. Colonel Carlson intends to stop the young bucks once and for all. He sent for Badger and recalled all the troops."

"Hell," Fargo said. It was becoming his favorite expression.

"The colonel has already taken their chief prisoner," Sadie said. "What else can he do?"

"Look for the renegades."

"A needle in a haystack," Sadie said. "He'd be wasting his time."

"He has to do something, all the people they're killing."

"The Bannocks know the country better than he does. They'll give him the slip."

"Whose side are you on?"

"My own."

Fargo grinned and tipped the bottle in a salute. "A gal after my own heart."

Sadie drank more beer. "I'd like to do what I can to help out. I'm thinking of going to the fort and offering my services."

"Colonel Carlson made it plain he doesn't want us around," Fargo reminded her.

"I'm worried about what he might do," Sadie said. "He's taking nearly his entire command out in the morning. There will barely be enough soldiers left to guard the post."

"You don't say."

Sadie downed the rest of her beer and pushed back her chair. "Care to join me?"

"No, thanks," Fargo said. He had something else to do. Something that could get him thrown in prison, or killed.

# 16

Fargo sat drinking until California finished playing cards and joined him. He explained what he had in mind, and the old scout chuckled.

"You ornery bastard. Count me in."

"It's too dangerous," Fargo said.

"As if that would stop me," California said in indignation. "We're pards, ain't we? How many times have we risked our hides for each other? Remember the Mountains of No Return?"

"I won't have you behind bars because of me."

"You at least need a lookout, and I won't take no for an answer."

They finished the bottle, collected their mounts, and rode off into the woods. The first clearing they came to, they made camp for the night. Neither cared to take a room in the settlement. Given a choice between the sky over their heads or a roof, they'd choose the sky ten times out of ten.

The night was clear, the forest quiet save for the occasional howl of a wolf or the yip of a coyote. Once a mountain lion screamed, and later the roar of a grizzly wavered on the wind.

To Fargo they were as ordinary as the rattle of a water pipe or the creak of a floorboard to a settler. He lay on his back, propped on his saddle, until sleep finally claimed him. He didn't stir until his internal clock woke him at the crack of the new day, as it nearly always did. He was up before California and had coffee brewing.

His friend liked to sleep with a blanket over his head. Now he poked it out, squinted, and smacked his lips.

Running a hand through his hair, which stuck out like so many spikes, he mumbled, "Morning, pard."

Fargo grunted.

"You still have your mind set?"

"I do."

"The army will be mad at us."

"At me," Fargo said. "And only if I'm caught. You're the lookout. You don't take part."

Scratching himself, California sat up. "Have you met him before?"

"Never set eyes on him until the other day."

"Then why in tarnation go to so much trouble?"

Fargo looked at him. "You know why."

California frowned, and nodded. "I reckon I do, at that. Sure wish I could see Colonel Carlson's face when he finds out. He's apt to have a conniption."

"It would serve him right," Fargo said.

Casting off his blanket, California jammed on his hat. "Someone else might not take too kindly to it, either. And he worries me more than Colonel Carlson."

"Who?" Fargo asked, even though he'd already guessed.

"Emmett Badger. Carlson picked him personally to be his scout. Go against Carlson and Badger might take it as you are going against him."

"Too bad." Fargo opened his saddlebag and took out his tin cup.

"I wouldn't want Badger mad at me. He's a hellion when he's riled."

"Makes two of us."

California rubbed his hands together. "I reckon I shouldn't fret over milk that ain't been spilt yet. Besides, in the dark you can slip in and out easy as can be."

"I'm not waiting a whole day," Fargo said.

In the act of scratching his stubble, California Jim paused. "You aim to do it before nightfall? In broad daylight?"

"No reason why not." Fargo put his hand close to the pot. It was almost hot enough.

"Have you gone loco? There will still be boys in blue there."

"Can't be helped," Fargo said. "I won't let them hang him when he has no say. And maybe he'll agree to lead his people out of the Salt Range until things calm down."

"I get it," California said. "If the rest of the Panati leave, the young bucks will go with them. But they'll come back eventually. At best, you're delaying things."

"It will stop the killing for a while and that's all that matters."

A couple of cups of coffee, a handful of pemmican, and Fargo was ready to light a shuck. He avoided the open valley floor by following the tree line. When they were abreast of Fort Carlson, he drew rein in the shadow of a towering pine.

The post bustled with activity. Soldiers were forming up, horses were being saddled, pack animals were being readied.

"Busy bees," California said.

It was pushing nine o'clock when the column departed. Colonel Carlson was at the head. On either side were figures in buckskin.

"One must be Badger but who's the other?" California said.

"Sadie said she was offering her services."

"Even after the Bannocks tried to stick arrows in her yesterday?"

"Some people forgive and forget easier than most," Fargo said.

Their accoutrements rattling, their horses raising swirls of dust, the troopers neared the far end of the long valley.

"I hope to hell Carlson doesn't start a full-fledged war," California muttered.

That wouldn't happen if Fargo could help it. And he was about to take the first step to prevent it. "Let's go."

"They're not out of sight yet."

"The sooner we get him to his village . . ." Fargo said, and let it go at that.

Acting as innocent as newborns, they made for the post at a leisurely walk.

"I want you to know, pard, that if we wind up in front of a firing squad, I won't hold it against you."

The sentry let them go by with a wave. Several wives were near the headquarters building, talking and gazing after the column. A trooper was over by the blacksmith's.

Fargo drew rein at the sutler's. His boots barely touched the ground when an officer strode out and looked them up and down.

"Gentlemen. I believe I saw you here the other day."

"You might have," California Jim said. "We had a palaver with your colonel."

"Who is on his way to thrash the Bannocks. I'm Captain Mathews. I'm in charge until Colonel Carlson returns."

"Pleased to make your acquaintance," California Jim said.

"Might I inquire what you are doing back? I was under the impression the colonel had no need of more scouts."

Fargo answered before California could. "We're looking for Sagebrush Sadie."

"You just missed her," Captain Mathews said. "She rode out with the detachment."

"She's scouting for them?" California said.

"What else?"

"But you just said . . ." California began.

Captain Mathews smiled. "Ah. You're wondering why the colonel asked her to join him, and not you. She's a special case."

"Because she's female," California said.

"Oh, no, not that." Mathews seemed about to explain but he noticed the women over by headquarters, one of whom was beckoning. He touched his hat brim. "If you'll excuse me, gentlemen, I see my wife needs me." He strode on past.

"What the hell is special about Sadie?" California wondered.

Fargo was more interested in the guardhouse. A trooper was leaning against the wall, his carbine in the crook of his arm.

California lowered his voice. "I still don't see how in hell you're going to do it with that bluebelly there."

"Watch and learn."

Fargo entered the sutler's. Two women were examining bolts of cloth, and the sutler himself was behind the counter, counting coins. Fargo went down an aisle to a display of hats and bonnets. Hoping it was big enough to fit, he chose a floppy hat with a wide brim.

"Do you want a blanket too?" California asked. "He can throw it over his shoulders."

"And have him stand out like a sore thumb?" Fargo shook his head.

The sutler looked up from his counting. "You're buying a new hat?" He regarded Fargo's own. "I'll probably lose the sale but yours looks perfectly fine."

"A man can never have enough hats," Fargo said.

"If you say so."

Fargo paid and walked out. At the rail he said, "This is as far as you go. Give a holler if you think anyone suspects."

"I hope he's worth it, pard."

The captain and the ladies had gone into headquarters. The soldier at the blacksmith's had disappeared, too.

Plastering a smile on his face, Fargo strolled toward the guardhouse.

The trooper guarding the prisoner straightened and moved in front of the door. "What can I do for you, mister?"

"I'm supposed to give this to Lone Bear," Fargo said, holding out the hat.

"What in hell for?"

"You saw me talking to the captain, didn't you?" Fargo asked.

"Sure did. But—"

"Mathews thinks that if he's nice to the Indian, the chief might cooperate. Give him a present and he might give the captain information about the renegades."

"Why'd he send you and not come himself?"

"His wife needed him," Fargo said. That much, at least, was true.

Gnawing his lip, the soldier glanced toward headquarters.

"Go ask him yourself if you want," Fargo said.

"No need, I reckon." The trooper fished a key ring from a pocket and inserted a key into the lock. "Just toss the hat."

"That wouldn't be friendly."

And before the trooper could stop him, Fargo walked in.

Lone Bear was seated cross-legged along the opposite wall, his arms folded. "You have come back."

"Brought you something," Fargo said, and dropped the hat in front of him.

"I not wear white man's clothes."

"Put it on anyway," Fargo said, "and I'll get you out of here."

"How you do that?"

Fargo turned and called out to the guard.

The private entered. "What is it, mister? That old redskin giving you a hard time?"

"No," Fargo said, and slugged him.

# 17

As he swung, Fargo felt a twinge of conscience. The soldier was only doing his duty. But a lot of people on both sides would die unless he took steps to prevent it, and the first step was to free Lone Bear. His punch caught the trooper flush on the jaw and felled him in his tracks.

Quickly, Fargo bent and pressed a finger to the guard's throat to be sure the pulse was steady. When Fargo straightened, Lone Bear was staring at him in undisguised astonishment.

"Let's go."

The Bannock leader went on staring.

"I'm getting you out of here," Fargo explained.

"You hit blue coat for me?"

"So you can escape."

"Why?"

Fargo had no time for this. Another soldier could stroll by at any moment. "We'll talk on the trail. We have to light a shuck."

"Light . . . what?"

"We have to go." Fargo gripped the old man's arm. "Now."

Lone Bear didn't move. "Why you help me? I not know you."

"By helping you I help your people."

"You not know my people."

"Damn it," Fargo said. He was close to losing his temper. "While you sit there being pigheaded, Colonel Carlson is leading his men into the mountain. What happens if they find your village?"

"It far away."

"He has two of the best scouts alive helping him," Fargo said. "Are you willing to chance that they won't?" He pulled on Lone Bear's arm but again the Bannock leader refused to move.

"Why you care what happen to my people. You are a white man."

Fargo almost slugged *him*. "If the colonel attacks your village, women and kids could die."

"They Panati women, Panati young. Not white women, not white young."

Fargo couldn't think of what to say that would convince the man he was sincere.

"How I know this not trick?"

"I just knocked out your guard. The army will throw me in here with you if they catch me."

"Maybe other one have hand in this."

"I came in here alone."

"You think I not know but I do."

Fargo grabbed the hat and shook it. "I don't know what the hell you're talking about and I don't care. Put this on. Tuck your hair up under it and walk with me to the sutler's. I'll climb on my horse, you climb on behind me, and we're out of here."

"Why I wear hat?"

"To hide your hair and your face. I bought it just for you to use," Fargo said, and shoved it at him.

Lone Bear examined it. He turned it over and ran a hand along the brim. "Good hat."

"Keep it if you want. It's yours." Fargo moved to the doorway and peered out. So far no troopers were anywhere near the guardhouse. "Our luck is holding. Come on."

Lone Bear was still admiring the hat. "You really let me keep hat?"

"Only if you get up off your ass right this minute," Fargo said.

Lone Bear stared and then said a strange thing. "You have soft heart."

Fargo shook his head. "I have no such thing. Now get over here."

To his relief, the old Bannock placed the hat on his head and stood.

"Tuck your hair up," Fargo directed. "From a distance the blue coats might mistake you for a scout."

"Tuck up?" Lone Bear said uncertainly.

Fargo showed him.

Grunting, Lone Bear did the rest himself. A few strands hung to his shoulders but most of it was now under the hat. "How that?"

"You could pass for a white man."

"I not insult you," Lone Bear said. "You not insult me."

"God in heaven," Fargo said, and stepped out, pulling the Bannock after him.

Lone Bear moved as slow as molasses. Taking a deep breath, he gazed at the sky and out across the valley, and smiled. "It good day."

"It might be your last if you don't light a fire in your leggings," Fargo warned.

"Fire . . . in leggings?" Lone Bear looked down at himself. "Why I want to burn me?"

"Forget it. We need to hurry." Fargo moved faster but abruptly slowed when the soldier who had been down at the blacksmith's earlier came out of it and crossed toward the barracks.

"We run for horse?" Lone Bear said.

"No. Act casual. And keep your head down so he can't see your face."

Lone Bear tucked his chin to his chest. "How this?"

"Beautiful," Fargo said.

"I not woman," Lone Bear said. "I man."

California Jim was leaning on the hitch rail and keeping an eye on the headquarters building. He suddenly straightened and gestured.

Fargo looked.

Captain Mathews and the women were coming out. Mathews and his wife were arm in arm and she was laughing at something he'd said. The captain was smiling. Then he looked across the compound and his smile faded.

"Uh-oh," Fargo said.

"What that mean?" Lone Bear asked.

"Run like hell for the Ovaro."

"Ov-what?"

"The horse that looks like a pinto."

"Me like pintos. They pretty horses."

"Run, damn it."

Captain Mathews chose that moment to point at them and holler, "You there! Stand where you are!"

"Hell in a basket." Fargo hooked an arm around Lone Bear and propelled him toward the sutler's.

The soldier crossing the parade ground stopped and looked in their direction.

Mathews bellowed, "Stop those two, someone!"

Fargo was moving as fast as he could. So was Lone Bear. That was the problem. Lone Bear wasn't as spry as he used to be.

At the hitch rail, California Jim vaulted onto his mount and wheeled it around, the Ovaro's reins in his hand. A jab of his heels and he trotted to meet them.

"Stop them!" Captain Mathews shouted.

A pair of troopers barreled out of the barracks, one pulling a boot on, the other donning a shirt.

"Stop them!"

The soldier over at the parade ground fumbled at the flap to his holster. Jerking his revolver free, he cried, "Halt or I'll fire!"

Soldiers were notoriously poor shots. Few used firearms before they enlisted, and once in uniform they didn't get to use them much, either. Cartridges cost money, and the army, always looking for ways to cut expenses, limited target practice to once or twice a month, and only a few rounds at a time. It was a wonder troopers could hit anything.

Still, when the soldier's revolver boomed, Fargo involuntarily flinched. A lucky hit was as deadly as a well-aimed shot.

"They not happy we leave," Lone Bear said.

Whooping with excitement, California Jim brought his horse and the Ovaro to a stop. "Climb on, pard," he bawled.

Fargo didn't need the urging. He vaulted onto the Ovaro, bent, and offered his arm to Lone Bear.

The old warrior stared. "You have big hand, white man."

"Grab hold, damn you."

Another shot galvanized the old Bannock into action. He gripped Fargo's forearm, and nodded.

Surprised at how light he was, Fargo swung him up and behind. "Hang on," he commanded as he reined sharply to the west.

The revolver cracked a third time and lead buzzed his ear. Hunching forward, he used his spurs.

Captain Mathews was shouting like a madman. Soldiers were rushing from several buildings but as yet none had a rifle.

The sutler emerged, turning a startled gaze on Fargo and California Jim as they raced by.

California did more whooping and waved his hat in the air.

"Your friend happy we be shot at," Lone Bear said in Fargo's ear.

Fargo swore. They had a lot of open ground to cover to reach the woods, and the few remaining soldiers would soon be in pursuit.

Cackling merrily, California came alongside. "That was slick as could be, pard."

"It could have been slicker," Fargo yelled to be heard above the pounding of hooves.

"There's never a dull moment with you," California said. "I never know what you're going to pull next."

Fargo glanced back. A dozen or more troopers were converging on the stable.

"But this stunt beats all," California continued. "Breaking a prisoner out. Next you'll be robbing banks." He cackled louder.

Fargo didn't find it at all hilarious. The army brass would take a dim view of his latest escapade. Yes, he had friends in high places, a few generals and colonels and majors he'd scouted for. But unless he could prove that breaking Lone Bear out was in the army's best interests, he'd end up in a stockade. Or worse.

"You have good horse," Lone Bear said.

"I think so."

"Him strong. Carry both of us. And him fast. Him be fine warhorse. You want trade?"

"No."

"Me give you five horses for him."

"No."

"Me give you ten horses."

"No."

"Me give you ten horses and one of my women."

"No, damn it."

"Why you mad?" Lone Bear asked.

"I'm not mad," Fargo lied. "We just need to reach those slopes before the soldiers come after us."

Lone Bear shifted and pointed toward Fort Carlson.

"Blue coats already after us."

# 18

Captain Mathews and fully a dozen soldiers were flying from the fort. Some had saddles on their horses. Others had jumped on in haste and didn't. With Mathews yelling and waving his arm as if it were a sword, they poured across the valley floor.

California Jim laughed.

Mathews struck Fargo as the dogged sort who would chase them to the gates of hell if he had to. Lashing his reins, he sought to reach the forest well ahead of them.

"Five horses and two women," Lone Bear said.

"You can't have the Ovaro," Fargo said for what he hoped was the last time.

"Now you sound more mad."

"I'm not goddamn mad," Fargo fumed. He slapped his legs and gave thanks they were far enough ahead it was unlikely the soldiers would shoot.

As if to mock him, rifles banged.

California Jim laughed and waved at their pursuers. He was having the time of his life.

"Whites strange," Lone Bear said.

"You don't know the half of it," Fargo said without thinking.

"Whites only half strange?"

"Do me a favor and don't talk. I have riding to do."

"Panati ride and talk at same time."

Another rifle shot cracked but it was the last for a while. The troopers didn't have lead to waste.

The forest loomed closer. Fargo was already thinking

of how he would shake the boys in blue once he reached it. "Which way to your village?" he asked over his shoulder.

"On horse is good," Lone Bear said.

"No. Which direction is it? East, west, north, or south."

"Go where sun rise."

"East it is," Fargo said, nodding. "How long will it take to get there?"

"Four sleeps."

Four days. Fargo could make it in half that by riding hell-bent for leather and sleeping only a few hours each night.

Relief washed over him when the woodland swallowed them. Drawing rein, he checked on the troopers. Still in dogged pursuit, they had fallen a quarter mile behind and some of their horses were flagging.

"We won't have to worry about them," California Jim declared.

"Don't count your chickens," Fargo said, and headed up the mountain.

"Where chickens?" Lone Bear asked.

"There aren't any," Fargo explained. "It was a figure of speech."

"What that?"

"Words that mean something other than what you think they mean."

"Whites very strange," Lone Bear said.

"Let's not get ahead of ourselves. Now hush up."

"We ahead of your friend."

"No, not that kind of ahead."

"You mean head on shoulders?"

"No."

"There is another head?"

"Do me a favor," Fargo said. "Don't say anything more or *my* head will explode."

An hour later they were so far above the valley floor, the soldiers below were the size of ants.

Fargo halted on a shelf, had the chief slide off, and did the same.

"That was fun," California Jim said, joining them. "We should do it again real soon."

Fargo sighed, took his canteen, and sat on a boulder overlooking the tiered slopes. Opening it, he gratefully swallowed, then offered some to the others.

"Don't mind if I do," California said.

Captain Mathews and the seven or eight troopers still with him had stopped in a clearing. Mathews took out a spyglass and trained it on the shelf.

Fargo waved.

His knees popping, Lone Bear sat cross-legged and regarded him with curiosity. "Why you try help my people?" he asked.

"Not that again. I already told you," Fargo said. "For the women and the kids."

"You think blue coats hurt them?"

California answered before Fargo could. "They might not intend to. But when Colonel Carlson surrounds your village and gives the order to close in, all it will take is for one warrior to resist and all hell will break loose. In the confusion . . ." He shrugged.

"Why whites make Panati hurt?"

"You're a fine one to talk," California Jim said. "It's your young warriors who went on the warpath."

"They do it for Smells Like Rose."

"They're counting coup for a squaw?" California smacked his leg. "I should have known. It's always the blamed women who get us in hot water."

Fargo motioned for silence. Down below, Captain Mathews and the troopers were turning back. Mathews was the last to wheel, and only after he raised his fist and shook it.

"Looks like you made a new friend," California said.

Fargo leaned back and contemplated the old Bannock. "You'll have to guide us. Are you sure you remember how to get there?"

"Panati not forget where lodge is," Lone Bear said indignantly.

California snorted. "They forgot there are more blue coats than there are blades of grass on the prairie."

"Many blue coats, yes," Lone Bear said. "Good fighters, no. Whites easy to kill."

"I'd like to see you try to kill us," California said.

"You different," Lone Bear said, and nodded at Fargo. "Him different. You like Indian."

"Carlson has a lot of soldiers with a lot of rifles," Fargo said. "They'll charge through your village shooting everything that moves."

"They shoot women? And children?"

"It's been known to happen," Fargo stressed. "Unless you want that, get us to your village as fast as you can."

It finally seemed to sink in. Lone Bear grew thoughtful, and urged them to get under way even before the horses were rested.

Instead of stopping at sunset as he'd ordinarily do, Fargo pressed on until near midnight. They kindled a small fire, had coffee and jerky, and crawled under their blankets.

Before daybreak they were up and saddled. Another grueling day of difficult riding saw them deeper in the Salt Range than Fargo had ever been.

This was the kind of raw country he liked. Where no white men had ever set foot. Where virgin forest had never rung to the chop of an axe. Where the streams were crystal pure. Where the wildlife hadn't been killed off for the supper pot.

Stark peaks rose miles higher, overlooking verdant valleys untouched by the plow. Deer thrived, and in the high meadows elk bugled.

It was creation as God meant it to be, untrammeled by that two-legged destroyer, man.

Fargo wasn't the only one who thought so.

"This is beautiful country," California Jim commented that night as they sat drinking coffee and chewing jerky.

"Panati country," Lone Bear said proudly.

"No sign of Colonel Carlson anywhere," Fargo mentioned.

"Maybe we're worried over nothing," California said. "Maybe he won't find the village."

"You're forgetting Badger," Fargo said.

"Good point," California said.

"Badger?" Lone Bear said. "Badgers only bite when you poke in hole."

"Not the critter, the scout," California said. "He's as good as Skye, here. If anyone can find that village of yours, it's him."

"Me remember now," Lone Bear said. "Scout with hard eyes."

"That's Badger, all right," California said.

"Sadie is with them, too," Fargo brought up.

"She's good but she can't hold a candle to Badger," California said. "If it was just her, we wouldn't have to go to all this bother."

"Maybe my people see them before they see us," Lone Bear said. "Maybe my people kill all blue coats."

"You better hope not," California said. "Nothing makes the army madder than a massacre. Wipe out Carlson and his command, and the army will send another officer with twice as many soldiers with orders to wipe you and yours out."

Lone Bear sighed. "Killing all whites know."

"Your warriors killed warriors from other tribes long before we came along."

"Kill enemy how we count coup," Lone Bear said.

"It's also how colonels like Carlson become generals," California said. He turned to Fargo. "It's a damn strange world, ain't it, pard?"

Fargo grunted. He'd done more than his share of life-taking. But it wasn't as if he'd set out to make it his life's goal. Were it up to him, he'd get along peaceably with everybody. A silly notion, since the real world wasn't peaceable. The real world was lead slugs and barbed arrows. The real world was cold steel and lances.

It was kill or be killed, and he'd be damned if he'd roll over for anyone. "Talk about something else."

California blinked. "Whatever you say."

"We should talk bears," Lone Bear said.

"Because you were named after one?"

"Bears kill," Lone Bear said.

"So do rattlers and wolves and mountain lions," California recited. "Hell, a bull elk will kill you if you get too close. Buffs charge if they so much as catch your scent. When it comes to killing, animals are just like us."

"Bears big. Bears have claws. Bears have teeth."

California snorted. "Painters have claws and teeth, too. Talking about bears is liking talking about goats. There's no point to it."

"You want bear kill you?"

"You're plumb ridiculous," California said. "I don't want anything to kill me. Anything or anyone. I intend to go on being cantankerous until I'm a hundred and ten."

"Maybe bear kill anyway."

Fargo reached for the coffeepot to refill his cup. "Why do you keep bringing up bears?"

Long Bear pointed across the clearing. "Because bear looking at us."

# 19

The Bannock said it so calmly, so casually, that Fargo expected to see a black bear. Since they rarely attacked humans, it was no cause for alarm.

But there, at the edge of the firelight, stood a massive monster that dwarfed any black bear ever born. The huge head, the high hump on its front shoulders, the brown hair with silver tips—it was a grizzly, and as they turned, it growled and rose onto its hind legs.

"Good God," California Jim blurted.

"Don't anyone move," Fargo cautioned. Their guns would be of little use. His Henry, while powerful enough to drop a buck or a hostile, would do little more than annoy a griz that size.

Towering gigantic in the starlight, the bear sniffed and rumbled deep in its enormous chest.

California Jim sat with his mouth agape, making no attempt to hide his fear.

Fargo hoped the bear would decide they weren't worth eating, and go on its way.

Suddenly Lone Bear rose. Facing the behemoth, he spread his arms, smiled, and commenced to sing in his own tongue.

"Quiet, damn you," California hissed.

Lone Bear paid no heed. He went on smiling and singing a chant that rose and fell like the swells on a Pacific shore.

Fargo braced for an attack. His best bet was to grab the Henry and jump on the Ovaro and get the hell out of there. He glanced at the horses. Unlike the Bannock, they had the good sense to stand perfectly still even though California's was quaking.

The grizzly tilted its head, its glowing eyes fixed on Lone Bear who began to slowly move his arms up and down.

"You consarned idiot," California snapped.

The grizzly looked at him and growled, then went on staring fixedly at Lone Bear.

Fargo had never seen the like. The bear acted half mesmerized.

Without any forewarning, the grizzly suddenly dropped onto all fours. It was so immense, so heavy, that its front paws striking the ground sounded like hammer blows.

Lone Bear's smile widened and he chanted at the top of his lungs.

Inexplicably, amazingly, the grizzly wheeled and melted into the night.

Fargo stared after it, listening, but heard nothing to mark its passage. It might as well be a ghost. He worried it might circle and come at them from another direction, as bears sometimes did.

Lone Bear stopped singing and lowered his arms. "Brother gone."

"You almost got us killed, you loon," California said. "What in hell were you thinking?"

"Me sang to brother," Lone Bear said. "Told him we are friends."

"Brother to a griz?" California scoffed.

"Me named after one."

"So what?" California said. "I'm named after a state but you don't see me singing to it."

Lone Bear seemed to choose his words with care. "My spirit . . . bear's spirit . . . all one. We brothers. Do you not see?"

"All I see," California said, "is that it's a damned miracle you didn't end up as bear shit."

"You white. You not understand."

"I savvy Indian ways as good as any white man," California said.

Fargo shut out their spat. Someone had to stay alert in case the griz returned. He wasn't convinced it wouldn't until a roar rose in the distance. It echoed and reechoed off the high peaks so that it seemed a legion of bears was on the loose.

At his suggestion they turned in so they could be up early and on the go.

A pink blush painted the eastern horizon when Fargo opened his eyes. He put coffee on and nudged his friend with his boot.

Lone Bear was already awake. "Maybe see brother today," he said hopefully.

Fargo knew he wasn't referring to another Bannock. "Let's not push our luck."

"Brother not harm us."

From under California's blanket came a grumbled, "Here we go again."

"Let it drop," Fargo said.

"Tell that to him."

They sat drinking coffee, California sullen and surly, Lone Bear smiling at the world.

Fargo was eager to get under way. He snatched up his saddle blanket and turned to the horses, and stopped cold. "Oh hell."

California swiveled. Cursing furiously, he leaped to his feet. "My horse is gone!"

The chestnut's hobble lay where Fargo had last seen the animal standing. He went over and scoured for sign.

"The Bannocks took him, I bet," California said, with a hard glace at Lone Bear. "They slipped in while we were sleeping and snuck away with him."

"Why didn't they take my horse, too?" Fargo said. Or, for that matter, slit their throats. He examined the hobble; it hadn't been cut. "Are you sure this was tight enough?"

"I know how to hobble a horse," California said petulantly.

Tracks showed where the chestnut had wandered off into the woods.

"I'll go after him," Fargo said, and hurriedly saddled

the Ovaro. As he was about to climb on, he spied gray tendrils rising into the sky to the south.

California spotted them, too. "Smoke," he said. "Four or five campfires. It must be the colonel. Not more than a mile off, I reckon."

Fargo swore. He'd counted on being far ahead by now. "I'll be back as quick as I can."

The chestnut had made a beeline through the trees as if it had somewhere to go.

At least, Fargo saw, it had been moving away from the soldiers.

For the next hour he pressed hard. He was midway down a rocky slope when he spied it in a valley below. It had stopped near a stand of cottonwoods and was drinking from a small stream.

Thinking it was a shame he didn't eat horse meat, Fargo descended and drew rein in the shadowed cover of some pines.

The moment he showed himself, the chestnut might run off. To avoid having to chase it all over creation, he dismounted, tied the Ovaro, and snaked into the high grass in a crouch.

Every ten feet or so Fargo raised his head to confirm the chestnut was still there. He was almost close enough to rush it when he raised his head a final time and heard a light chuckle.

"Fancy running into you here."

Fargo straightened. Only then did he see that a rope had been thrown over the chestnut's neck and the other end wrapped around a cottonwood.

Leaning against it was Sagebrush Sadie, her rifle propped against her leg, her arms across her chest. "Are you trying to catch flies with your mouth hanging open like that?" she teased.

"I'll be damned," Fargo said. Movement in the stand showed him where her own horse was tied.

"I don't blame you for being surprised," Sadie said. "I sure am. What in hell are you doing here?"

"Trying to catch California's horse."

"I reckoned it was his," Sadie said. "But the last I saw of you two, you were in Salt Creek."

Fargo went to the chestnut and patted it. "We're obliged for you catching him."

"Catch, hell," Sadie said. "I was on a scout for Colonel Carlson and came to this valley and there it was, right where you see it."

"We're still obliged," Fargo said. "I'd better get it back. California wasn't any too happy that it slipped its hobble."

"Hold on there," Sadie said, straightening. "You still haven't said what you're doing here."

Fargo decided to tell the truth, to a degree. "The same thing you are. We're looking for the Bannock village."

"What for?" Sadie asked. "You're not doing it for Carlson."

"On our own account," Fargo said, and went to slide her rope off.

"Hold on," Sadie said again. "You still haven't told me why."

"We'd like to stop the killing if we can," Fargo hedged.

"How? By riding into their village and asking pretty please for the renegades to stop shedding white blood?"

"I haven't thought that far ahead."

Sadie straightened, her brow puckered. "That's not like you. You think more than anybody I know. It's why you're usually two steps ahead of everybody else."

"I really do have to be going." Fargo was anxious to get out of there before Carlson and the soldiers showed up. "Where is the good colonel, anyhow?"

Sadie jerked a thumb to the west. "About half a mile back. He's moving slow and careful so as not to give the hostiles any warning."

"And then what?"

"He won't tell me what he's up to. All he says is that he's going to solve the hostile problem once and for all."

"I don't like the sound of that."

"Me either. It's why I practically begged him to let me come along. I have friends among the Bannocks. I don't want them to come to harm."

"We think alike," Fargo said.

"Isn't this sweet?" a gravelly voice said, and out of the cottonwoods rode Emmett Badger. Drawing rein, he leaned on his saddle horn and stared at the chestnut. "California is here too?"

Fargo motioned. "We're camped up the mountain a ways. His horse ran off and I came to find it."

"I heard what you two bleeding hearts just said," Badger remarked, giving Sadie a resentful look.

"All I want is to stop the killing," Fargo said, suppressing his temper.

Badger's hard countenance grew harder. "Who in hell do you think you are?"

"Emmett," Sadie said.

"Butt out," Badger snapped. He jabbed a finger at Fargo. "I asked you a question. Who do you think you are, interfering in army matters?"

Fargo didn't answer.

"*I'm* the scout at Fort Carlson. Not you. If anyone has a say, it's me. And I say whatever the army wants to do, we stay out of it."

"I'm worried that Carlson plans to attack the Bannock village," Fargo confessed.

"Well, guess what," Badger said. "He does."

# 20

Sagebrush Sadie put a hand to her throat. "You know this for a fact?"

"Out of his own mouth," Badger said, "before we left the fort."

"You didn't try to talk him out of it?" Fargo asked.

"Why should I? I don't make army policy. It's just this one band that's acting up. Colonel Carlson figures to put them in their place."

"There are women and children in that village," Fargo said.

"If they stay out of the way, they won't be hurt."

Sadie bowed her head and said, "I didn't reckon on this. They'll be upset with me and I can't blame them."

"Who?" Badger said.

Fargo had heard enough. He must reach the village before Carlson. He slid the rope off the chestnut and was about to climb on and ride it to the Ovaro when Badger brought his own mount over, blocking his way.

"Where do you think you're going?"

"I told you," Fargo said. "To take California's horse to him."

"He can wait. You're going to stay right here until the colonel shows up."

"Like hell," Fargo said.

"There's something fishy you showing up like this," Badger said. "I think you're up to no good, and I'm keeping you here so the colonel can sort it out."

"Don't do this," Sadie said.

"I told you before to butt out," Badger snapped. "Injun lover," he added.

Sagebrush Sadie blushed.

"So the rumors are true."

"What rumors?" Fargo asked.

"About little miss scout here," Badger said, but he didn't elaborate.

"You think you know but you don't," Sadie said. "There's more to it."

"I don't give a good damn," Badger said. "All I care about is doing my job." He smiled a cold smile and said to Fargo, "Which is why you're staying put."

Fargo turned from the chestnut. "Let's talk this out."

"Nothing you can say or do will change my mind."

Fargo took a step and held his hands out in appeal. "I'm asking you to do me a favor and pretend you didn't see me."

"And then what? You hurry off and warn the Bannocks that the colonel is coming?"

"Only a handful of warriors have gone on the warpath. Not the whole village."

"This is war, and in war you attack an enemy where it hurts them the most."

"Damn it, Badger. The women. The kids."

"The warriors who are killing whites have squaws who feed them and shelter them and kids they're raising to be just like them."

"So they should suffer too?"

"What about all the whites who have suffered? All the white women and kids who have been massacred?"

"It doesn't make attacking the village the right thing to do."

Badger shook his head in disgust. "I never took you for a weak sister. It shows how little we really know each other."

Sadie said, "Please, Badger. Let him and me get the women and children out of there."

"How will you do that without the warriors finding

out?" Badger shook his head again. "You must think I was born yesterday."

Fargo took another half step. He would try one last time. "Tell me something, and be honest." He paused. "Is there any chance at all that I can talk Carlson into surrounding the village and take the Bannocks prisoner without harming them?"

"Not a snowball's chance in hell."

"It would stop the killing."

"The renegades might not even be there."

"All the more reason not to attack."

Badger bent toward him. "The renegades need to know that when they kill whites, their own people suffer. Maybe then they'll think twice about killing any more of us."

"It's like being in quicksand," Sadie said. "Nothing I do can stop me from going under."

Badger glanced at her in annoyance. "What in hell are you talking about?"

Fargo had tried. Honestly tried. Badger and he didn't always see eye to eye but he liked the man, and didn't want to do what he did next: he sprang, grabbed Badger's leg, wrenched it from the stirrup before Badger could react, and tumbled him from the saddle.

He darted around Badger's horse to get to him before Badger could stand but he'd forgotten how uncannily quick the man was.

Already in a crouch, his knife in his hand, Badger hissed, "You son of a bitch."

Fargo went for his Colt. He didn't intend to kill Badger, only to wound him. But as he cleared leather Badger leaped and kicked. The impact sent the Colt spinning from his grasp. Fargo backpedaled and Badger's blade narrowly missed cutting him open.

"Stop it! Please!" Sadie cried. "This has gotten out of hand."

Neither Fargo nor Badger so much as glanced at her. Badger wagged his knife in circles, his eyes twin daggers.

"Make it easy on yourself. Sit down and keep your

hands where I can see them and we'll wait for the colonel."

"I can't do that," Fargo said.

"Then it's you and me," Badger said, and came at him fast and low.

Badger thrust and Fargo sidestepped. He kicked at Badger's face, only to have Badger dodge and grab his boot and wrench. Unbalanced, he fell onto his side. As he hit, he rolled. Pushing to his feet, he palmed the toothpick.

Fargo was forced to give way as the other scout unleashed a dazzling display of glittering steel. It was all he could do to keep from being stabbed or slashed. Badger was good, damn good, as good as he was.

Twisting, shifting, countering, always in sinuous motion, they were so intent on each other that they didn't realize how close they were to the edge of the bank.

"Look out!" Sadie tried to warn them.

Fargo felt the ground give way. He threw himself aside and sought purchase for his boots but there was none to be had. He dropped like a rock.

The water was six inches deep, if that. He got some in his mouth and nose and sputtered as he rose.

"For God's sake, stop the fight!" Sadie pleaded.

Badger surprised Fargo by saying, "It doesn't have to be like this."

"It does unless you're willing to let us warn the village."

"I can't do that."

"And I can't let women and kids die."

"Suit yourself."

Badger feinted, half spun, and stabbed at Fargo's ribs. Fargo blocked, did a spin of his own, and felt his blade bite flesh.

Badger retreated out of reach and stared at scarlet rivulets running along his forearm. "You're the first to ever cut me."

Fargo was given no time to reply. Badger flew at him

as if possessed. He was forced to give way and backed into water that rose midway to his knees. Badger grinned, and he knew Badger had done it on purpose.

Badger pretended to feint, and Fargo's counterthrust met empty air. There was a stinging sensation in his left thigh, and now he had scarlet spreading down his buckskins.

"Time to get this over with," Badger said.

Fargo coiled. Badger came straight at him and drove blood-flecked steel at his throat. Instinctively, he whipped the toothpick up to block. He didn't see Badger's foot rising but he felt the kick that connected with his side and damn near fractured a rib. Recoiling, he held the toothpick in front of him to keep Badger at bay. But the other scout did a strange thing; he dropped onto his free arm and swung his body in a blur. Badger's legs slammed into the back of Fargo's, sweeping Fargo's legs out from under him. Before Fargo could even think to try to recover, he was on his back, his head above the water.

Badger swept in. Fargo stiffened as his neck pricked to the sting of the tip of the other's knife.

"Twitch and you die."

Fargo turned to stone.

"Drop your knife."

Fargo did.

"I don't want to kill you, Skye," Badger said.

Fargo didn't reply. Any movement of his throat might drive the knife deeper.

"I want you to promise that you'll sit here and wait for Colonel Carlson."

Fargo yearned to rise up, to continue their fight. He couldn't remember the last time he'd been whipped.

Badger applied pressure to his blade. "I don't hear you."

"You'd take me at my word?"

"You're like me. When I give my word, I keep it. No matter what." Badger paused. "Now, is it yes or no?"

"I give my word," Fargo said, and grew hot all over at the humiliation.

Badger chuckled and stood. "That wasn't so bad, was it? I'll get a fire going and we'll have some coffee while we wait."

Sagebrush Sadie cleared her throat. "You're forgetting about me."

"Not likely," Badger said. "You'll wait here with us."

"Like hell," Sadie said, and went for her six-gun.

# 21

Emmett Badger had his knife in his gun hand. Sadie probably thought she could draw before he could drop the knife and go for his Colt. She was wrong. His Colt was out and pointed at her before she cleared leather.

Sadie did as Fargo had done—she imitated stone.

"That was plain dumb," Badger said as his knife thwacked the ground at his feet.

Flushing red, Sadie took her hand off her revolver. "I suppose you want me to give my word, too."

"No," Badger said.

"Why not?"

"I don't trust you."

Her flush deepened. "He's a man so him you trust. I'm female, so me you don't."

"No," Badger said. "I trust him because I've never heard tell of him breaking his word. I don't trust you because you're a conniving bitch."

"Why, you miserable—" Sadie balled her fists and took a step.

Badger cocked his Colt, stopping her in her tracks. "If you think I won't shoot, you're mistaken. Fargo wouldn't, because he treats women with respect. Me, I'd as soon gun a female as a male."

"Ain't you something?" Sadie said.

"Go ahead. Rile me. That's real smart." Badger motioned. "Unbuckle your gun belt, careful-like. Give me an excuse to squeeze this trigger and I by-God will."

As Sadie pried at her buckle, she snapped, "You're one of *those*, aren't you? A hater of everything female."

"Don't put words in my mouth," Badger said. "I just think you have no business pretending to be a man."

"What?"

"You heard me. Scouting is man's work. No matter how good you get, you'll always be half the scout most men can be."

"Goddamn you." Sadie looked at Fargo. "Did you hear him? This is exactly what I was talking about the other night. It's why I have to work three times as hard to get half as much work. How fair is that?"

"Need a shoulder to cry on?" Badger taunted. "Maybe Skye will let you bawl on his."

Sadie was a volcano about to explode. "I hate you," she declared.

"I'll try not to lose sleep over it." Badger gestured. "Why is that gun belt still around your waist? You don't have all day."

With sharp, angry movements, Sadie cast it to the ground. "Happy now?"

"Take a seat next to Skye."

Sulking, Sadie came over and sank down. "If it's the last thing I ever do, I'll see you pay for this."

"Do you see my knees shaking?" Badger said.

Fargo was thinking about the Bannocks, and what he could say to convince Colonel Carlson to change his mind.

Sadie tore out a handful of grass and threw it at the water. "I reckon this has gone on long enough."

Both Fargo and Badger said at the time, "What?"

"He's held off because I told him not to do anything, but now I have no choice." Sadie sighed. "I'd hoped that I wouldn't have to show my hand."

"What in hell are you babbling about now?" Badger demanded.

Sadie turned to Fargo. "Do you speak much Bannock?"

"Not much at all. Why?"

She looked at Badger. "How about you, woman-hater? You've been at Fort Carlson a while. You must have picked some up."

"A few words here and there," Badger said. "Is there a point to this?"

"Only that neither of you will have any idea what I'm saying," Sadie said, and raising her voice, she called out in the Bannock tongue.

"What are you up to?" Badger demanded.

The answer came in the form of a whizzing shaft. It streaked out of the cottonwoods and buried itself in Badger's back with a fleshy *thwack*. He was knocked forward and arched his spine, staring in disbelief at the barbed tip jutting from his chest. Then, without uttering a sound, he pitched to his knees and fell onto his side.

Sadie laughed.

Fargo started to rise but a tall Bannock, his face painted for war, strode out of the cottonwoods with another arrow notched to the bowstring and trained on him.

It was Thunder Hawk.

Again Sadie said something in the Bannock language. "I told him not to kill you," she translated.

"Friend of yours?" Fargo said.

"Lover."

"Oh hell."

"His name is Thunder Hawk." Sadie introduced him, unaware that Fargo had already encountered him. Rising, she stepped over to the Bannock and put an arm around his waist. "He's the reason all this is happening."

Thunder Hawk was naked from the waist up. He was well muscled, and when he looked at her his eyes said things his mouth never would unless they were alone.

"Care to enlighten me?" Fargo asked.

Sadie was about to respond when a rumble from the far end of the valley caused her to jerk her head up. "Carlson is closer than I thought." Frowning, she scooped up her gun belt. "I should let Thunder Hawk kill you. He killed the other two. But I believe you when you say you want to help the Bannocks. So do I. It's only fair, seeing as how they're helping me."

"I'm in the dark here."

"I don't have time to explain. I have to go warn the

Bannocks about the colonel." Sadie hurried to her horse and climbed on.

Fargo stared at the unwavering barbed arrowhead, and stayed where he was.

Sadie appeared to be wrestling with an internal conflict. She gnawed her lip. She looked up the valley. She looked down the valley. Finally she leaned on her saddle horn. "Listen, as soon as I'm gone, get on your horse and light a shuck for anywhere you want. The Snake River country. The Green River country. Anywhere but here."

Fargo didn't say anything.

"This isn't over yet, and I'd hate for my friends to kill you, too. So please. I'm begging you. Get out of here and don't come back." Sadie drew her revolver, pointed it at him, and cocked it.

"Change your mind?"

She said something to Thunder Hawk, who lowered his bow and dashed into the cottonwoods.

"You fixing to shoot me?" If she was, Fargo would be damned if he'd go down without trying all in his power to kill her first.

"Not unless you make me," Sadie said. She let out a long breath. "God, this is such a mess. I should have stopped it somehow. But I guess, secretly, I wanted it as much as they wanted to do it for me."

"If riddles were gold, you'd be rich."

"You'll figure it out," Sadie said. "When you do, don't hold it against me."

"Jed Crow and Tennessee and Badger might."

"Yeah, well," Sadie said.

Hooves drummed, and around the stand came Thunder Hawk on a fine warhorse. He stopped next to her and said something, and when she shook her head, spoke sternly to her.

"He says," Sadie translated, "that he is letting you live. But only because I want him to."

"If you want my thanks, don't hold your breath."

"He says that you should take my advice and go. If you stay, he'll count coup on you as he has the others."

Fargo gave Thunder Hawk a cold smile. "Tell the son of a bitch he's welcome to try."

Sadie raised her reins. "This is good-bye, I hope. It's for your own good to go."

The rumble up the valley had grown louder. Sadie listened a moment, then addressed Thunder Hawk in his own tongue and the pair galloped off in the other direction, Thunder Hawk looking back as if he expected Fargo to try something.

Fargo might have, too. But just then Emmett Badger groaned.

Kneeling, Fargo rolled him onto his side. He felt for a pulse and found one, weak, but steady. "Tough as hell," he said.

Badger's eyes fluttered, and he coughed. "My ma didn't raise puny sons." He looked at the barbed tip. "Who?" he asked.

"A Bannock with the handle of Thunder Hawk," Fargo said. "A friend of Sadie's."

"Take it out."

"You should wait for the colonel," Fargo suggested. There might be a medical officer with the column.

"What the hell for?" Badger grimaced. "It isn't as if you haven't done this before."

Yes, Fargo had dug out his share of arrows, but still. "It's awful close to your heart. Taking it out could kill you."

"Leaving it in will kill me, too."

"Hell," Fargo said. Bending, he inspected where the arrow had entered Badger's back. Carefully wrapping his left hand around the shaft, he gripped the arrow near the feathers with his other hand. "Ready?"

"Just do it, damn it." Badger grit his teeth.

"On three," Fargo said, and braced himself. "One. Two." As he said three, he applied all his strength in a powerful wrench that snapped the feathered end off as neatly as if it were a dry stick. He tried not to let the arrow move but it was impossible to hold it completely steady.

Badger let out a hiss and a groan, and sagged.

Fargo threw the piece aside. "You sure about the rest

of it? A doc could do it and give you something for the pain."

"Stop dawdling." Badger swallowed. "One thing, though. If I die, kill the warrior who did it."

Fargo thought of Jed Crow and Tennessee. "I aim to anyway." He rose and moved around in front and knelt. "Here comes the hard part."

"Get it done." Badger set himself and clenched his jaw.

Fargo gripped the arrow close to the tip. It was slick with blood. He wiped his hand on the grass and gripped it again. Bunching his shoulders, he said, "Here we go," and slowly began to pull. Sometimes arrows didn't cooperate and had to be dug out; this one slid out as easily as he could hope.

Badger shook, and swore. "That wasn't so bad," he claimed.

"I'll patch you up," Fargo offered.

"Before you do," Badger said weakly, "one more thing."

"You want to save the arrow as a keepsake?"

"No," Badger said. "I want you to kill Sagebrush Sadie, too."

# 22

Fargo was halfway up the mountain, leading the chestnut, when the column swept into the valley and clattered along the creek. He drew rein to watch.

Emmett Badger was where he'd left him, and weakly waved an arm to get their attention.

At a barked command from Colonel Carlson, the troopers came to a halt. The colonel was the first off his mount and at the scout's side.

Tending to Badger would delay Carlson a while, giving Sadie and her friend time to reach the village and warn the Bannocks.

Fargo wasn't about to turn back, though. He had a score to settle. Gigging the Ovaro, he continued his ascent.

California Jim and Lone Bear were where he had left them, seated at a small fire, California drinking coffee, the Panati leader chewing on a piece of jerky California must have given him.

"Took you long enough, pard," California remarked with a chuckle. "You must have chased that critter plumb to Wyoming."

Fargo climbed down and poured himself some coffee. "We need to talk," he said, looking directly at the Bannock.

"You sound mad," Lone Bear said.

"Mad as hell," Fargo confirmed. "Tell me about Sagebrush Sadie."

Lone Bear frowned. "Oh," he said. "Her."

Fargo waited, and when the old warrior just sat there,

he prodded him with, "She told me that she lived with a tribe once. Was it yours?"

Almost reluctantly, Lone Bear said, "She first come our village one winter ago. She have good heart. We let her stay."

"And?" Fargo said when Lone Bear didn't go on.

"She meet warrior. She like him. Him like her. They spend all time together."

"Thunder Hawk," Fargo said.

"You know him?"

"I met the bastard."

"Not call him that," Lone Bear said. "Thunder Hawk my son."

Fargo straightened. "The hell you say."

"What's he got to do with anything?" California Jim interrupted.

"Thunder Hawk is the leader of the renegades," Fargo said. "He's to blame for Crow and Tennessee."

"Your own son?" California said to Lone Bear. "So that's why Colonel Carlson threw you in the guardhouse. To get your son to stop the killing."

Sorrow deepened the wrinkles on Lone Bear's aged face. "Me tell Thunder Hawk not kill whites. Me tell him it bad medicine."

"What's he trying to prove?" California asked. "He sure as hell can't lick the entire U.S. army."

"Him do it for her," Lone Bear said.

"For Sadie?" Fargo said.

Lone Bear grunted. "His head in whirl over her. Him do anything she want."

"Son of a bitch," Fargo growled. He saw it all, yet could hardly believe it. "You didn't try to stop them before they shed any blood?"

Lone Bear answered so quietly, they had to strain to hear him. "One day son come to me. Him say he go kill whites. Me say no, that whites leave us be, we leave whites be. Him not listen. Him and others attack what you call wagon train. Him kill other whites, too. All for her. For Sadie."

"So no one would suspect when she sent for us and Thunder Hawk started picking off her fellow scouts one by one," Fargo said.

"What's this?" California said.

"Sadie wrote the letters that brought us here," Fargo explained, "so Thunder Hawk could do us in."

"Sadie wants all of us dead? What on earth for?"

"We're men."

"How's that our fault?"

"With us out of the way, she figures she'll get a lot more work."

California's eyebrows tried to crawl up his forehead. "She's having us killed off to fill her poke?"

"More or less," Fargo said.

"Has that gal been chewing locoweed? I can't hardly believe it."

Fargo grunted. The notion *was* preposterous, but then people did preposterous things all the time.

"I'll have to hear it from her own lips," California said. "And even then . . ."

Draining his cup, Fargo stood. "Saddle up. We have some hard riding to do." And some hard killing, he almost added.

Lone Bear acted befuddled. At first he had them ride north but then he changed his mind and said it must be to the west and later he changed his mind again and said the village must be to the south.

Fargo went east. Soon they came to a ridge that overlooked a verdant valley. And there, winding away, was a long line of Indians on horseback and on foot.

"We found them, by-God," California Jim declared.

Lone Bear wasn't nearly as glad.

As was customary, the main body was made up mostly of older men and the women and children. Their lodges had been torn down, and along with their possessions, tied to travois being pulled by horses and dogs.

They were flanked by warriors in their prime, ready to ward off an attack.

Fargo rode down out of the tall timber and came up on

the exodus from the rear. Almost immediately a warrior spotted them and yipped a warning, and a dozen peeled away and charged to intercept them.

Drawing rein, Fargo shifted, gripped Lone Bear by the arm, and swung him off. Then he placed his hand on his Colt.

California had his rifle across his saddle. "They don't look none too friendly," he observed.

"Don't shoot unless I do," Fargo said, and bent toward Long Bear. "Whether we do or we don't is up to you. They start anything, a lot of women will mourn for their husbands tonight."

Lone Bear stepped in front of the Ovaro and spread his arms.

The warriors slowed.

Fargo willed himself to stay clam. One slip in judgment and there would be a bloodbath. "Nice and easy does it," he said.

"I hear you, pard," California replied.

Lone Bear greeted the warriors. A husky Bannock responded. By the end of their exchange, the expressions of the warriors were friendlier.

Lone Bear turned. "Me tell them how you take me from blue coats."

Fargo kept his hand on his Colt.

"Me say you friend. Me say you come warn them blue coats coming."

"Only Sadie and Thunder Hawk already did," Fargo said. "I want to know where they got to."

Lone Bear and the husky warrior talked some more. "They warn and go away."

"Which direction?"

Smiling, Lone Bear pointed to the south.

Fargo refrained from calling him a liar. He was Thunder Hawk's father, after all. "You'd best join your people. The blue coats aren't that far behind."

Lone Bear stepped to the husky warrior's mount and the man swung him up. "Me thank you," he said. "You like Sagebrush Sadie. You have good heart."

Fargo let that pass. He sat there as the Bannocks wheeled and rode to rejoin the exodus.

California grinned. "That went better than I reckoned it would."

"This is where we part company."

"Say that again?"

"The Bannocks aren't out of danger. Carlson might still catch up to them, and there could be a massacre. It's up to you to prevent it."

"How?"

"Simple. You tell him about Sadie and Thunder Hawk. Make it clear as you can that Thunder Hawk and his friends are behind the killings, and no one else. The rest of the Bannocks are innocent."

"He's liable to call me a liar to my face and I'll have to hit him."

"Tell him he'll hear it from Sadie herself if I can bring her in alive."

"I knew it. You're going after them and you don't want me along."

"It's best I do this alone."

"I'm not an infant, you know."

"Never said you were." Fargo raised his reins. "You're wasting time. Good luck."

"Give 'em hell, pard."

Fargo touched his spurs and didn't look back to see if California was doing as he asked.

Once he was above the valley, Fargo looped to the west. He figured the renegades—and Sadie—wouldn't bother hiding their sign. They didn't expect anyone to come after them.

Once he found their trail, he would stay after them until hell froze over. They had a lot to answer for, and he would damn well make sure they did.

As he searched, he climbed, so that when evening fell, he was miles above the valley, so high up that a vast vista of peaks and slopes stretched in all directions.

He made cold camp on an open bench where there was grass for the Ovaro.

Stars sparkled to life and the night came alive with roars and howls and shrieks.

Fargo sat and scanned the ink below and was rewarded with flares of light to the southeast. That had to be the Bannocks. Presently he saw more to the south; Colonel Carlson and the column.

He went on scanning. Eventually he would spot what he was looking for. Unless they'd made a cold camp, as he had.

Over an hour went by and he was beginning to think he was out of luck when he spied a solitary fire to the southwest.

It was small, and well hidden from prying eyes, except from above.

"Got you," Fargo said.

Pulling his blanket tight around him, he curled on his side and was asleep within moments. The chill wind, the chorus of bestial cries, were as a lullaby to a civilized townsman. He slept soundly until near the crack of the new day, and was in the saddle with the blush of the rising sun.

Time to begin settling scores.

# 23

It was the middle of the morning when Fargo found where they had camped. Tracks of unshod horses and moccasin prints confirmed they were Bannocks. He made it out to be nine warriors.

A single set of shod hoofprints showed that a white was with them.

Sagebrush Sadie and her lover had headed out early, to the south.

Fargo didn't push to catch up. He had a long, hard track ahead. It wouldn't do to ride the stallion into the ground.

When he did overtake them, he had no illusions about whose side Sadie would take.

He was glad California Jim was with the soldiers. He could count on two hands the number of truly good friends he had, and California was one of them. He liked the old scout, liked him a lot, and would hate for him to come to harm.

He'd seen a lot of killing in his time, done for every reason under the sun. Greed, lust, hatred, or for the sheer thrill of killing.

This was a new one. He kept thinking there had to be more to it than Sadie killing off her competition. He'd like to find out what before it was all over.

He reminded himself there were no depths people wouldn't plumb.

Put in terms of the wilds around him, when all was said and done, the human animal was the most vicious of all. When it came to sheer, wanton savagery, the two-legged wolves of the world beat their four-legged counterparts all hollow.

Fargo wondered if he should include himself. After all, he'd done more than a little killing in his time. Almost always in self-defense or to protect others. He wasn't a cold-blooded murderer. Although in this instance, he had no intention of turning Thunder Hawk and the other hostiles over to Colonel Carlson. The army would throw them into prison for the rest of their lives, which some might say was fitting.

Not him. Why should they go on living when they'd denied life to so many men, women, and children.

That last was abominable; women and children. An enemy out for your hide was one thing. Innocents who had never done anyone harm, another. It was why he'd gone to warn the Bannocks about Carlson. Their women and children didn't deserve to suffer for the atrocities Thunder Hawk and his friends committed.

He would see to it that justice was done. Some might say he didn't have the right to set himself as judge, jury, and executioner. But that wasn't it at all. He was setting right their wrongs by avenging those who couldn't avenge themselves.

Fancy words, but it all came down to one thing. He was going to kill the sons of bitches.

Along about noon Fargo stopped to rest the Ovaro. His quarry was still heading south. Toward the fort. Toward the settlement. That worried him. With most of the troopers out in the field searching for them, the smart thing for the renegades to do was find a hidey-hole and lie low for a spell. Instead, it appeared they were out to add more victims to their list.

And then it hit him. There were barely two dozen soldiers left at Fort Carlson. It could be that Thunder Hawk was going to do unto the colonel as the colonel had planned to do unto the Bannocks.

Fargo picked up the pace. He was still a day and a half out, with a lot of rugged terrain to cover.

To cut that down, he rode until midnight, slept barely

four hours, and was on the move in the dark before sunrise.

He kept telling himself it couldn't be. Attacks on military posts were rare. But Thunder Hawk knew a skeleton force had been left, and it would boost his prestige among his tribe. A warrior who attacked a *fort*. The Bannocks would sing his praises around their fires for many winters to come.

Fargo was almost to Salt Valley when he spied vultures. He also saw ribbons of smoke rising toward the carrion eaters.

"No," Fargo spoke for the first time since parting company with California Jim, and brought the Ovaro to a gallop.

Even though he suspected the renegades were long gone, he shucked the Henry from his saddle scabbard as he neared the fort and levered a cartridge into the chamber.

"No," he said again.

The headquarters, the barracks, the guardhouse, and another building had been burned to the ground. All that were left were charred timbers.

Bodies were sprawled everywhere; soldiers, women, and a child who had tried to flee across the parade ground.

Fargo felt an icy fist close on his chest. At the same time, his veins filled with molten fire.

The sutler's still stood, and smoke was rising from the chimney. Two troopers were on the front porch, one at either end, and when the near one saw him, the man let out a yell.

As Fargo drew rein, Captain Mathews emerged.

Faces pressed to the windows—other soldiers, women, children.

Mathews was hatless and his uniform was smudged and torn, his face that of a man who had been through hell and back again.

"You," he said.

"Which way did they go?"

"South," Mathews said, and gazed out across the carnage. "They snuck through the grass and hit us so hard and so fast—" He stopped. "I never thought they'd attack the fort. I wasn't prepared—" He stopped, and swallowed, and said softly, "God."

"They won't get away with it." Fargo raised his reins.

"Hold on." Mathews straightened. "I should take you into custody for what you did."

"You won't."

"What makes you so damn sure?"

Fargo gestured. "This."

Mathews gazed at the bodies again, and seemed to age ten years. "I got as many as I could save into the sutler's. There are gun ports. We were able to hold them off."

"It was the best you could do."

Mathews looked at him. "Have you seen any sign of the colonel?"

"If he took my advice he's on his way back," Fargo said. "He should be here in two or three days."

"That old Indian," Mathews said, "he had nothing to do with this, did he?"

"No."

Now it was Mathews who gestured. "Did they do this because they thought we had him locked up?"

"The ones who did this did it because they like to kill whites. Plain and simple."

"Hell," Mathews said. He clenched his fists. "I can spare a trooper to go with you."

"They might circle back. You'll need every man you have."

Mathews managed a wan smile. "Give those bastards hell."

Fargo reined around. A vulture was alighting near the dead child, its wings spread wide to slow its descent. Snapping the Henry to his shoulder, he aimed and squeezed. At the blast, the bird did an ungainly flop onto its back, flapped wildly a bit, and was still.

"We should have seen to the bodies," Mathews said. "I was worried the savages were waiting for us to show ourselves."

With a nod, Fargo departed. He was thinking of the

settlement, Salt Creek, and the men, women, and children who called it home. They'd be easy pickings. Easier, even, than the soldiers.

The fresh tracks of the war party were easy to follow.

Halfway to the settlement, the Bannocks had gone off into the trees. Fargo stuck to the pitiful excuse for a road, making good time.

It was a pleasant surprise to round the last bend and behold everything as it should be: a few people in the street, horses dozing at the hitch rails, a dog nosing at a barrel, a chicken taking a dust bath.

Fargo took the Henry with him into the saloon. The barman nodded and went on wiping the counter. Three locals were playing poker.

At a corner table sat Bear River Tom, a nearly empty whiskey bottle in front of him, his arms around a pair of plump ladies whose bodices threatened to burst at the seams. "Well, look who it is!" Tom heartily roared. "Where have you been, pup?"

Fargo crossed to the table. "I could ask the same about you."

Bear River Tom bobbed his head at the lady on the right and the lady on the left. "I have been up to my eyebrows in tits."

The women laughed.

"Ain't he a caution?" the one on the right said.

"I never met a man so fond of my jugs," the other dove declared.

Tom removed his arms from their shoulders and smacked the table. "Have a seat, why don't you? There are plenty of tits to go around."

Hooking a chair with a toe, Fargo pulled it out. "While you've been sucking teat, a lot has gone on."

"I'm all ears," Tom said with a grin.

The grin faded as Fargo filled him in.

"Damnation," Bear River Tom said, and helped himself to the last of his coffin varnish. "I should have been with you and California. When will I learn? Some things are more important than tits."

"You didn't think that last night," the woman on the right said.

"I never saw a man fit two in his mouth at once," the other woman said.

Tom looked at them in annoyance. "I never thought I would say this, but enough about tits. Why don't you ladies go buy some tit perfume or something while we have us a talk."

The dove on the right snickered. "Tit perfume?"

"That was sweat, honey," the other one said.

Bear River Tom smacked each on the fanny as she went by. Then he leaned on the table and said gruffly, "Sadie killing scouts. It's the craziest thing I ever heard."

Fargo was toying with the notion of buying a bottle but decided not to.

"You're going out after them?" Bear River Tom wanted to know.

"Need you ask?"

Bear River Tom stood. "Then what are we waiting for? I liked Jed Crow. Tennessee, too. I'm coming, and I won't take no for an answer."

Fargo led the way out. He pushed through the batwings and Tom pushed through after him and they stepped to the edge of the overhang.

"I can't wait to kill me some hostiles," Bear River Tom said eagerly.

Fargo went to step to the Ovaro, and stiffened.

A rifle barrel was pointed at them from the corner of the general store across the street.

# 24

Fargo dived at Bear River Tom and heard Tom's bleat of surprise even as the rifle boomed. He heard the slug smack the front of the saloon behind where Tom had been standing.

"What the hell?" Tom roared.

Pushing to his feet, Fargo snapped off a shot from the Henry. Chips flew from the corner of the store and the rifle barrel disappeared. Working the lever, he skirted the hitch rail.

People were yelling and pointing and coming out of buildings.

Fargo reached the general store and peered around before committing himself. He glimpsed a figure with long black hair and leggings, and jerked back as the figure's rifle boomed.

That glimpse had been enough to tell him who it was: Thunder Hawk. The rifle, unless he missed his guess, was Sagebrush Sadie's.

Boots drummed, and Bear River Tom joined him. "Who the blazes shot at you?"

"At you, not me," Fargo set him straight, and told him who it was.

"The hell you say!" Tom cried, and before Fargo could stop him, he was around the corner and flying toward the rear.

"Damn it," Fargo said, and ran after him.

Bear River Tom reached the far end, glanced both ways, and plunged into the forest.

"Tom, wait!" Fargo hollered, but he was wasting his

breath. It was a mistake to rush in blindly but he did it anyway. He didn't want the tit-crazed fool to share the fate of Tennessee and Jed Crow.

"Where are you, damn you, you skulking savage!" Bear River Tom bellowed, somewhere ahead.

"Tom, hold up!" Fargo tried once more. Tom, of course, didn't. The crackle and snap of underbrush guided his steps, but suddenly they stopped and the woods fell quiet.

Fargo dug in his heels. Crouching, he sought some hint of movement. The wind had died and not so much as a leaf stirred.

Back in Salt Creek people were yelling and raising a ruckus. Here, everything was deathly still.

Fargo grew uneasy for Tom. It could be his friend had blundered into an ambush. Against his better judgment he eased forward.

Without warning, a shape reared. Fargo swiveled and trained the Henry but relaxed his finger just in time. "You damned lunkhead," he growled. "You almost got yourself shot."

"I lost him," Bear River Tom said in frustration, peering intently into the forest. "I wasn't more than a stone's throw back and he gave me the slip."

"We'll pick up his trail," Fargo vowed. "And when we find him, we'll find her."

"Sadie," Tom said. "I still can't hardly believe she is a party to this. And her a female, to boot."

It had been Fargo's experience that women can be as deadly as men and he said as much to Tom. "Don't make the mistake of thinking they can't."

"I know that," Bear River Tom said. "Injun gals in particular. Apaches, Comanches, Blackfeet women, you expect it from them. But Sadie is white."

Fargo didn't see what that had to do with anything, and told him so.

"I know white women can kill," Bear River Tom said. "Especially a gal like Sadie. She dresses and rides and shoots like a man. So naturally she kills like a man, too."

"I hadn't looked at it that way," Fargo said.

"If there's one thing I know," Bear River Tom declared, "it's females."

"I thought it was tits."

"Same thing."

They searched but couldn't find any trace of Thunder Hawk. Reluctantly, they headed back.

Fargo watched behind them, his thumb on the Henry's hammer.

"Relax, pup," Bear River Tom said. "He's long gone by now."

Nearly every soul in the settlement had gathered in front of the saloon. Almost all the men had guns. Mothers anxiously held their young ones.

Bear River Tom pushed on through and into the saloon, leaving Fargo to explain.

"So the savages are only after you scouts?" a man in a bowler said, sounding greatly relieved.

"None of us need to worry, then," another exclaimed, happy as could be.

"The hell you don't," Fargo said, and informed them of the attack on the fort, and that Colonel Carlson and most of the troopers were many miles to the north. "You need to post sentries," he advised. "And gather the women and children in one place where you can protect them better."

"To hell with that," a woman in a yellow bonnet said. "It's every person for him or her self. I'm taking my kids home and hiding in the root cellar until the soldiers show up."

Others shouted that they agreed with her, and before Fargo could stop them, the settlers scattered like chickens about to be swooped down on by a hawk.

Fargo called after them but in less than two minutes he was the only one in the street. "Everywhere I go," he said to himself, "I run into jackasses."

A drink was called for. Just one, to wet his throat before he set out after Sadie and her lover.

The saloon was empty save for Bear River Tom, over

at the corner table sucking down bug juice. "Mabel and Martha have gone into hiding," he lamented, "and took their tits with them."

Fargo went behind the bar, selected an unopened bottle of Monongahela, and brought it over.

"How soon do we head out?" Tom asked.

"Fifteen minutes," Fargo said. That should be enough to convince the Bannocks no one was after them.

"Do you reckon on asking some of these sheep to go with us?"

"I wouldn't take them if they paid me."

"Good," Tom said. "We'd only have to hold their hands, anyway." He chugged and wiped his mouth with his sleeve. "Doesn't it make you mad?"

"The sheep?"

"No. We were being stalked and none of us knew it." Tom scowled. "I've heard of a crazy bastard who went around strangling women. And an outlaw who went around killing every tin star he saw. And I've known a few who liked to kill blacks and redskins. But I never heard of a scout-killer before."

"Your point?"

"We have to put a stop to it."

Fargo stared.

"I know. That goes without saying. But it's not just Thunder Hawk and his pards, is it?"

"No," Fargo said glumly.

"And *that's* my point. I'm not Badger. I can't kill anybody, anywhere, anytime. I have—what do they call 'em?—scruples."

Fargo swallowed more whiskey. So did he. He just hid them real well.

"I ain't a woman killer," Bear River Tom went on. "Blowing out a female's wick is an awful waste of tits."

Smothering a snort, Fargo nearly choked on the rotgut.

"Well, it is," Tom insisted. "And the bad part of all this is that the tits belong to Sadie." He angrily thumped the table. "I like her, Skye. I like her a lot."

"So did I," Fargo said.

"But she has to be held to account. For Jed Crow. For Tennessee. For that arrow Thunder Hawk stuck into Badger. Hell, for everything her lover has done."

"I know."

"The thing is," Bear River Tom said, almost in a whisper, "I don't know if I can. I get her in my gun sights, I'm not sure I can squeeze the trigger."

"Maybe you should stay."

"And leave you to go up against them alone?" Tom shook his head. "Not on your life. We're brothers in buckskins, and friends besides."

"Brothers in buckskins?"

"Like it? I just made it up." Tom grinned, but it immediately faded. "Which would make Sadie our sister in buckskins, wouldn't it?"

"When we catch up to them, I'll deal with her."

"You have it in you? You can look her in the eye and do what has to be done?"

"Maybe she'll make it easy," Fargo said uneasily. "Maybe she'll try to kill us."

"And if she doesn't? If she leaves it up to her red boyfriend?"

"I'll cross that bridge when I come to it," was the best Fargo could come up with.

"Don't count on me to cross it with you. I'm only saying all this now so I don't let you down later. If I hesitate, it could get us both killed."

"You're a considerate bastard," Fargo said.

Bear River Tom laughed. "Mostly I'm a horn toad. When a woman jiggles her tits at me, I'm clay in her hands."

They lapsed into a moody silence that lasted until Fargo pushed his chair back and stood.

"Time?" Bear River Tom said, and took a last quick gulp. "I reckon I'm as ready as I'll ever be."

No one was abroad. The good people of Salt Creek were shuttered in their homes and their businesses.

"You see this?" Bear River Tom said, with a sweep of

his arm at the empty street. "This is the difference between civilized folks and us."

"We're not civilized?" Fargo said as he stepped to the Ovaro.

"Not deep down, no. We like life rough and wild and free. We should have been born back when every man was a law to himself. When if someone looked at you cross-wise, you could pull out a sword and hack them in half."

"Is it me," Fargo said, forking leather, "or have you had too much to drink?"

"I'm serious," Bear River Tom declared, and swung onto his own mount. "I should have been born one of those barbarians they talk about. Had me a harem of dancing girls. All of them naked from the waist up. All those tits to drool over."

"I knew it," Fargo said.

"What?"

"Everything comes back to tits with you."

"The only tits I'm thinking about now are Sadie's, and whether we're up to putting a bullet between them."

Fargo crossed the street and rode along the general store and into the woods. Together they roved for a sign, and it was Tom who found it—the tracks of a single unshod horse.

"Thunder Hawk was alone when he took that shot at us," Tom realized.

"Let's go find him," Fargo said, "and return the favor."

"Don't forget about Sadie."

"No way in hell," Fargo said.

# 25

Two days.

Two days they had been at it and still were far behind those they were after.

Fargo had a hunch that Sadie and Thunder Hawk knew he was after them and were fanning the breeze to the south. That in itself bothered him. Why go south, when it was wiser for them to head north, toward Canada, into country no white man had ever set foot in? Or west, into untracked wastes that had never seen the rut of a wagon wheel? South would eventually take them to the Green River country, to the Oregon Trail, to where they were bound to run into a lot of whites.

Fargo scowled. He'd been thinking too much of late, and thinking at the wrong time could get a man killed.

Bear River Tom was in a sullen funk. Whether because of Sadie or some other cause, he didn't say.

Fargo decided to find out when they stopped at midday to rest their horses.

Tom was slow to climb down. He moved to a log and sat, his chin in his hands.

"What's eating you?" Fargo got right to the point.

"I'm fine."

"Bull. You haven't mentioned tits once since we left Salt Creek."

Tom poked at the dirt with his toe. "Don't you ever get tired of it?"

"Of tits?"

"Why do you keep bringing them up?" Tom shook his

head. "No. Tired of the killing. We see a lot of it, the job we do. Doesn't it ever get to you?"

"I try not to think of it," Fargo said. Occasionally, though, he'd remember—bodies riddled with bullets, men who had been scalped, men and women who had been gutted or mutilated in a hundred different ways, freighters tied to wagon wheels and fires lit under them, a trapper who had been skinned alive. On and on it went.

"When my time comes no one will miss me."

"Not that," Fargo said.

"I'm feeling sorry for myself, I know," Bear River Tom said. "But look at Crow and Tennessee. We planted them, and that was that."

"That's all there ever is."

"I'd like to think I'll be missed. That at least one person in this world will toast my memory."

The way Fargo saw it, life was hard, sure, so a man had to be harder. But to bring Tom out of his mood he said, "I'll toast it with California every now and then."

"You'd do that for me?" Tom beamed. "I'm grateful. I have a bad feeling about this. Like my tit days are about over."

Just what Fargo needed. He was counting on Tom to back him when they caught up to the hostiles. But the shape Tom was in, he'd be of little use.

"I can tell by that look you think I'm making a fuss over nothing."

"Feelings don't always amount to much."

"I hope to God you're right."

As the hours passed and the miles fell behind them, Fargo kept hoping Tom would come out of himself. But the next day Tom was the same. And the day after that.

They neared the end of the Salt Range.

It was a bright morning, and they were descending a series of slopes that would bring them to the flatlands.

Ahead grew blue spruce mixed with pines. Finches were flitting about, and somewhere a magpie screeched.

The hoofprints of the nine warriors, and Sadie, were plain enough that a ten-year-old could track them.

A last incline littered with boulders was all that separated Fargo and Bear River Tom from the shadowed boles of the spruce and pines.

The Ovaro raised its head.

Instantly, Fargo drew rein. He trusted the stallion's instincts more than he trusted his own. "Hold up," he cautioned.

Bear River Tom drew rein next to him. "What is it?" he asked.

"I don't—" Fargo began.

Arrows streaked out of the woods, half a dozen or more, all let fly at once.

Fargo barely had time to haul on the reins and holler, "Hunt cover!" A shaft nicked his hat. Another creased his arm. A third struck his saddle inches from his leg, and glanced off.

Bear River Tom cursed, and banged off a shot. "Go!" he roared. "Go! Go! Go!"

Together they raced up the slope and into a belt of saplings. Bringing the Ovaro to a halt, Fargo vaulted down, yanked on the Henry, and ran back to where he could see their back trail. "Come and get it," he said, wedging the stock to his shoulder.

No one appeared.

Fargo stayed put. He was certain the renegades would try to finish them off. "Do you see any sign of them?"

When Bear River Tom didn't reply, Fargo turned.

Tom hadn't climbed down.

"What are you still doing up there?" Fargo demanded, and only then did he see the two arrows sticking out of him.

Fargo ran over and grasped a limp arm. "Can you hear me?"

Tom's eyes were shut, his teeth mashed together. "My ears work fine," he growled, "but I hurt like hell."

Fargo didn't wonder. One of the arrows was in Tom's left shoulder, the other jutting from between his ribs. Setting the Henry down, he reached up to ease Tom off.

"Forget about me. Go after them."

Fargo carefully lowered him to the grass and was about to sink to one knee when Tom raised his head, and pointed.

"Look out!"

Fargo whirled.

Three Bannocks were bounding toward them. Two had bows, the last a lance. A bowstring twanged and an arrow zinged but Fargo twisted and it missed.

A flick of his wrist, and the Colt molded to his hand. He fanned a shot, and the second bowman, about to let loose a shaft, buckled as if punched in the gut.

Not missing a heartbeat, Fargo fanned the Colt again. At the blast, the Bannock with the lance smashed to the earth.

That left the last one.

Fargo slapped the hammer twice, his finger curled around the trigger.

He thought that was all of them and went to turn to Bear River Tom. But the first warrior he'd shot had lunged upright and was coming at him wielding a knife. He shot the man again, and the Bannock stumbled but still didn't go down.

"Kill him," Tom cried.

Fargo sent a slug ripping through the warrior's forehead.

"Damn," Bear River Tom said. "They almost had you."

Quickly, Fargo reloaded. He was inserting the last cartridge into the cylinder when hooves rumbled lower down the mountain.

"The rest are heading for the hills," Bear River Tom gloated.

Or for the flatland, Fargo gauged, judging by the sound. "You should lie still."

"Why do they always say that to people who have been hurt? If a man is about to die, he should make the best of the time he has left."

Fargo performed some delicate probing. The arrow in Tom's shoulder wasn't life-threatening, and the one in his side had skimmed the rib cage. "You're one lucky buck-skin, brother."

"Two arrows sticking out of me, and I'm lucky? What do you call unlucky? Having my head chopped off?"

"They missed your vitals."

Bear River Tom shifted and bit his lip against the pain. "It sure doesn't feel like they did."

Fargo hiked his pant leg to get at the Arkansas tooth-pick. "I'll have them out in two shakes of a lamb's tail."

"The hell you will. You'll take your time and do it right. Sadie and her lover aren't going anywhere."

Yes, Fargo reflected, they were, and soon they'd be so far ahead it would take him days to catch up, if he ever did.

Nonetheless, Tom came first.

He gathered firewood and kindled a fire and put water from his canteen on to boil. He also used his whetstone on the toothpick.

Bear River Tom watched, a slow grin spreading across his face. "Do you know what this means?"

"Your premonition was wrong?"

"That my tit days aren't over."

"The women of the world are waiting in line."

"Scoff if you must, pup, but when I'm healed, I'm heading for Denver and Madame Colleen's House of a Thousand Delights." Tom chuckled, and grimaced. "I aim to fondle every damn tit in the place."

With a sigh, Fargo set to work. It took the better part of an hour to extract both shafts and clean and bandage the wounds. He used Tom's blanket for the bandages, which didn't sit well with Tom.

"I reckon we should use it since I'm the one who is hurt. But now I have to buy a new one."

"Poor baby."

Tom mopped at his pasty brow. "Has anyone ever told you that you have a mean streak?"

"It keeps me alive."

When it came time to ride on, Fargo hesitated. "Are you sure you can take care of yourself?"

"The hostiles are long gone. The worst I have to worry about are a meat-eaters, and I can handle them." He patted his rifle and his revolver.

"I'll be back as soon as I can," Fargo promised, and stood.

"I'm sorry to have to leave it up to you," Bear River Tom said.

"Taking care of the hostiles?"

"Taking care of Sadie," Tom said. "It shouldn't all be on you but that's how it's worked out."

"I'll do what I have to."

Fargo had lost enough time. Another moment, and he was in the saddle and in motion.

Bear River Tom hollered after him to be careful. He didn't answer. What else would he be?

By his reckoning there were six Bannocks left, including Thunder Hawk. Odds were they would try another ambush.

Would Sadie take part? In all the time he'd been wandering the West, he could count the number of women he'd had to shoot on one hand and have fingers left over. Could he shoot Sadie if she forced him to? She'd been a friend, after all. Hell, she'd been a lover.

Time would soon tell.

# 26

Fargo expected a single ambush.

The Bannocks had other ideas.

He was half a mile lower, dappled by the shadows of tall pines, a cushion of needles under the Ovaro's hooves muffling the thuds. His hand was on his Colt, and when a figure whooped and reared and let fly with a feathered shaft, he flashed the six-shooter out even as the shaft left the string. He fired and dived from the saddle and didn't see if his slug hit.

Landing hard, he heaved up and was ready to shoot but the figure wasn't there.

The Ovaro had gone a few yards and stopped. It looked back at him, unruffled by the gunfire it had heard so many, many times.

As Fargo started to rise, the stallion looked past him. He whirled, and damned if a painted warrior with a tomahawk wasn't stealthily stalking toward him. Their eyes met, and the warrior shrieked a war cry and attacked.

Fargo fired, sidestepped to avoid the other's rush, fired again.

The warrior splayed his fingers over his middle and slowly crumbled. The hatred in his glare was practically a blow in itself. He glared until his life ebbed, taking his hate with him into the afterlife.

Fargo heard thrashing and saw the vegetation shake where the bowman had been.

His aim had been true.

The Bannock was on his back, a stain spreading across his chest, his bow at his side, forgotten. He hissed through his teeth and spat in poor English, "We kill you yet, white dog."

"Nice to meet you, too," Fargo said. He was alert for others but it appeared to have been just these two.

"Me Wolf Running," the warrior hissed.

Fargo recollected the name. It was the warrior who was going to take Sophie Johnson into his lodge. "Soon you'll be Wolf Dead."

The warrior's hate was a mirror of the first man's. "Me count coup on many whites," he boasted.

"You can't take coup with you," Fargo said, slipping a cartridge from his belt to reload.

"You not live long," Wolf Running said. "Thunder Hawk kill you."

"He'll try."

"All white-eyes should die," Wolf Running snarled. Those were his last words. His mouth parted but only a long breath came out, and he was gone.

Fargo left the bodies for the scavengers. He'd be damned if he'd bury anyone who tried to kill him.

Now there were four, plus Sadie. It didn't help his nerves any to know that the next time they would plan it better.

Half an hour, and he was almost to the flatland. A last acre of slope ended in a low bluff that dropped off precipitously.

The bluff was too steep for the Ovaro. He'd have to go around. He reined wide, and stopped. It hit him that the bluff was perfect for the next ambush. They knew he'd have to go around, too. There was plenty of brush and timber. They could be anywhere.

Fargo looked to the right and caught movement out of the corner of his left eye.

A warrior had risen to his knees and was sighting down an arrow.

Fargo shifted and fired, and the Bannock reacted as if he'd been kicked. Fargo would have fired again but there was a sound above him and he glanced up to see a swarthy form hurtling out of a tree. He tried to bring the Colt up just as a battering ram caught him in the chest and slammed him from the saddle.

Fargo's vision blurred. For a few seconds he was helpless. The only thing that saved him was his knee; it jammed into the warrior's gut as they came down, and the warrior, too, was dazed.

The Bannock recovered and whipped his knife on high for a fatal stroke.

Fargo shot him between the eyes. The splatter of blood was nothing. He shoved the body off and sat up. Two more dead and he was still breathing.

Fargo slowly rose. He was hurting where the warrior had slammed into him. He moved to the Ovaro and placed his hand on the saddle horn.

Instinct caused him to spin.

Another warrior was almost on him. This one had an antler-hilted knife with a foot-long blade, and slashed at his throat. He dodged, went to shoot, and the warrior seized his wrist.

Fargo slugged him. Indians seldom used their fists. When they fought it was nearly always with weapons. Some tribes had friendly wrestling matches, but fisticuffs, beating another man to a pulp, was a white invention.

The Bannock was rocked onto his heels.

Fargo punched him again, and yet a third time, and if he didn't break the warrior's jaw it wasn't for a lack of trying. The grip on his wrist slackened. Tearing his arm free, he jammed the Colt's muzzle into the man's side and squeezed the trigger.

The young renegade stiffened. Blood burst from his mouth and nose. He said something, a few words that ended in a gasp. There was no hate on his face, only surprise.

Fargo took a deep breath to steady himself. He should be used to this by now, all the times others had sought to snuff his wick.

As he reloaded he gazed out across the flatland. Far in the distance, swirls of dust rose.

"Well, now," he said.

It made sense to go at a gallop, to catch them quickly and get it over with. He didn't. He rode at a fast walk.

Part of him wasn't in a hurry. Part of him wasn't looking forward to . . . her.

The flatland wasn't truly flat. Rolling swells of grass were broken here and there by hollows and buffalo wallows and an occasional hill.

Dust no longer rose but in a while something else did: a plume of smoke.

Fargo drew rein. He checked that every cylinder in the Colt held a cartridge. He slid the Henry from the scabbard and jacked the lever to feed a round into the chamber. The rifle in his left hand with the stock on his thigh, and the Colt and the reins in his right, he tapped his spurs.

She was seated in front of the fire, sipping coffee. Behind her was a small pond. Her horse was there, too.

Only her. Only it.

Fargo scowled. A rare sadness washed over him. He would play it out her way but he sincerely wished she hadn't brought them to this.

A prod of his knees, and Fargo cautiously approached.

He raked the ground around her, studied the pond and the reeds that grew at its edge, and gazed at a stand of trees a hundred yards away.

Sagebrush Sadie went on sipping until he came to a stop. "Hi, handsome."

"Where is he?" Fargo asked.

"He left me. Can you believe it? After he put me in this fix, he up and rode away."

"Did he now."

Sadie nodded. "He said that if you made it this far, he wanted no part of you. I wouldn't have thought he was yellow, but there it is."

"Thunder Hawk is a lot of things," Fargo said, "but a coward isn't one of them."

"A compliment from you? I reckoned you'd want him dead more than anything."

"He has much to answer for," Fargo said, "and so do you."

Sadie held the cup in both hands in her lap. "About that. Do you want to hear my story or not?"

Fargo wrapped the reins around the saddle horn and slid his boots from the stirrups but stayed in the saddle.

"I might as well."

"Good," Sadie said. "First off, we didn't plan it. It just sort of happened."

"A rainstorm sort of happens. A buffalo stampede sort of happens. Butchering women and children, no."

Sadie frowned. "Now see. You've already made up your mind. But let me tell you how it really was." She paused. "I lived with the Bannocks a spell. That's when him and me met. The moment I looked into his eyes, I know. You know how it goes."

"I know."

"He was a hothead. He'd go off and attack whites from time to time. I didn't like it but I cared for him too much to stop seeing him."

"True love," Fargo said.

"Don't be sarcastic. We both know he's not the only Indian who resents us whites for taking their land and trying to force them onto reservations."

"No," Fargo agreed, "he's not."

"So I can't hardly blame him, can I? Anyway, one night I was drinking and told him how upset it made me that the army favors male scouts over us females." Sadie uttered an odd little laugh. "He was the one came up with the idea of killing you and the others. I tried to talk him out of it but he said he was doing it for me, to show me how much he cared."

"There should be violin music," Fargo said.

"Don't be mean, damn you."

Fargo noticed that her horse had stopped grazing and was staring at the pond. "Tell me one thing," he said. "If you're so fond of him, why did you make love to me?"

Sadie giggled, of all things. "Curiosity, I suppose. You should hear the tales they tell about you. The great Skye Fargo. The man with the redwood in his pants. I wanted to see it for myself."

"So much for true love." Fargo hadn't taken his eyes off the pond. A lone reed had separated from the rest and was slowly moving closer.

Sadie patted the ground beside her. "Why don't you climb down and join me? Truth to tell, I wouldn't mind another poke by that pole of yours."

"My pole thanks you," Fargo said drily. "But blaming it all on Thunder Hawk won't wash."

"Why not?"

"Thunder Hawk didn't write the letters."

"Oh," Sadie said. "Those."

"And now you've set yourself out as bait," Fargo said. "He hasn't gone anywhere. He gave his horse a smack on the rump and sent it off into those trees. Then he cut a reed so he could breathe and he's in the pond waiting for me to climb down and turn my back so he can finish it."

Sadie went rigid.

"Him first, then," Fargo said, and fired the Henry into the water near the reed.

Almost instantly Thunder Hawk exploded out of the water, a knife in his hand. He took two dripping steps and cocked his arm to throw it.

Fargo sent a slug from the Colt into his right knee, and Thunder Hawk staggered. He recovered, raised his arm again, and Fargo shot him in the other knee. Pitching forward, Thunder Hawk glowered and opened his mouth to say something.

Fargo sent the last slug between his teeth.

Sagebrush Sadie hadn't moved. She stared at the ruin of her lover and a tear trickled down her cheek. "Well," she said, and set down the cup.

"It doesn't have to end like this," Fargo said. "You can turn yourself in."

"And be behind bars the rest of my days?" Sadie shook her head. "I like the wide-open spaces too much." Rising, she lowered her hand to her holster.

"Don't," Fargo said.

"Maybe one day you'll find it in your heart to forgive me."

"Damn you."

Sadie's hand stabbed for her revolver and Fargo fired his. In the silence that followed, he said quietly, "Rot in hell, bitch."

Shaking himself, Fargo holstered the Colt. He would take the bodies to Fort Carlson, collect California Jim and Bear River Tom, and spend a week in Denver drinking and womanizing and trying to forget.

Not that he ever would.

## LOOKING FORWARD!
### The following is the opening section of the next novel in the exciting Trailsman series from Signet:

### TRAILSMAN #375
### TEXAS SWAMP FEVER

*1861, the Texas swamp country—
where there are a hundred ways to die.*

If looks could kill, Skye Fargo would have been dead. He saw distrust and dislike on every face, in every glare.

A big man, wide at the shoulders and slim at the waist, he rode into Suttree's Landing with his right hand on his hip above his Colt. His lake blue eyes betrayed no more concern than if he was out for a stroll in a St. Louis park, but Suttree's Landing was a far cry from a civilized city like St. Louis. It was a backwater hamlet at the edge of the Archaletta Swamp, and the people were suspicious of strangers.

Fargo didn't care. He had a job to do, and any jackass who gave him trouble would find out the hard way he wasn't a cheek turner.

The Landing wasn't anything to brag about. Most of the people lived in shabby shacks that wouldn't have stood up to a strong prairie wind. But there wasn't much wind in the swamp, except when it stormed.

The general store, the hub of commerce for miles around, alone among all the buildings in the hamlet, had glass in its windows.

The people were a mix of white and half-bloods and a few Indians. Tame Indians, they were called, to set them apart from the wild ones that lived deep in the shadowed haunts of the vast swamp.

Sullen, sharp-eyed, the inhabitants watched Fargo and those behind him come down what passed for a street. On every face—even the children's—was the stamp of hardship and poverty.

Fargo drew rein at a hitch rail and dismounted.

Several locals were lounging against the wall and eyeing him much as hungry wolves might eye a buck. Unshaven and unkempt, they wore clothes that a St. Louis beggar wouldn't have been caught dead in.

One had a wad in his cheek and spat brown juice near the Ovaro's front hoof, which brought snickers from the others.

Fargo stared at the spitter until the he shifted his weight and frowned.

"I don't much like being looked at, mister," the spitter said.

"Spit at my horse again and you won't have a mouth to spit with."

The man smirked. "Is that right?"

Fargo placed his hand on his Colt. "It sure as hell is."

Some of the smug went out of the spitter. "You'd shoot a man who ain't heeled?" All he had around his waist was a middling-size knife.

"A man spits on my horse," Fargo said, "he has it coming."

"Here, now," said a beanpole in a shirt two sizes too small. "You can't just ride in and talk about shootin' folks."

"That's right," spoke up a heavyset brute with more

eyebrow than forehead. "Bodean can spit where he damn well pleases."

Their tone made Fargo bristle. "Anytime any of you reckon you are man enough," he said.

The beanpole straightened, and his thin lips curled back from yellow teeth. "Listen to you. You think you're the cock of the walk, don't you?"

"It's easy enough to find out."

By then the rest of Fargo's party had filed out of the woods and drawn rein. The lead rider, who sat ramrod straight in his saddle and didn't seem entirely comfortable in his store-bought suit, cleared his throat.

"That will be quite enough, if you please, Mr. Fargo. I'm sure these gentlemen meant no disrespect."

"Like hell they didn't," Fargo said.

The lead rider climbed down. Only a few inches over five feet, he carried himself as if he were taller. His boots were polished to a shine, and the revolver on his left hip was worn in a holster with a flap. He nodded at the swamp rats and said, "How do you do. I'm Ma—" Catching himself, he changed it to, "I'm James Davenport. Would this be Franklyn Suttree's establishment?"

"Franklyn?" the spitter said, and snorted. "Hereabouts we call him Sutty."

"Ain't you somethin'," the beanpole said, "in your fancy duds?"

"City boy," said the one with eyebrows like thick caterpillars.

Davenport wheeled on him. "I'm older than you, I'll have you know."

Fargo couldn't resist. "Take it easy," he said, and threw Davenport's remark back at him, "I'm sure these gentlemen meant no disrespect."

Just then another member of their party dismounted. Even taller than Fargo, he had arms as thick as tree trunks and a face that might have been forged on an anvil. He, too, wore a new store-bought suit. He, too, wore a flapped holster. "Is there a problem, sir?" he asked Davenport. "Say the word, and we'll deal with it."

"That won't be necessary, Mr. Morgan," Davenport said. The rest of their party was climbing down.

Fargo saw the three locals give a start and their mouths fall open, and he knew why without turning. The next moment he smelled her perfume and inwardly swore. He'd been against bringing her but the government had insisted she come.

"We've finally arrived," Clementine Purdy declared. "I swear it took us forever to get here." She had big green eyes and full red lips and a bosom that bulged farther than most. A bonnet contained brunette curls, and her shoes were of the finest calf leather.

"Hell, lady," Fargo responded in annoyance, "we haven't even started yet."

Davenport frowned. "Need I remind you that she *is* a lady, and an important one? I'll thank you to watch your language around her."

"Please," Clementine Purdy said. "Mr. Fargo may speak as he pleases."

"Not while I'm in charge," Davenport said.

Fargo noticed that Bodean and the other two were listening with keen interest.

"In charge of what, mister?" Bodean asked. "Who are you folks, anyhow?"

"We're a hunting party out of Galveston," Davenport said, feeding them a lie.

Fargo had warned the major that few if any of the locals would believe him, and he could see by the expressions on Bodean and his two friends that he had been right.

"You came all this way to hunt?" the beanpole said skeptically. "Ain't there any deer and bear around about Galveston?"

Davenport adopted a knowing smile. "If deer and bear were all we were after, we could have spared ourselves the trip. But we're after more dangerous game. A type that abounds in this great swamp of yours." He paused. "We're after alligators."

The beetling brows of the heavyset man met over his nose. "There's plenty of gators hereabouts, sure enough. But I never heard tell of folks comin' all the way from Galveston or anywhere else to hunt 'em."

"Damned peculiar," Bodean said.

"There's a first time for everything," Davenport cheerfully told them.

"Why in hell would you want to hunt gators?" the beanpole asked.

"I've hunted for years," Davenport said, expanding on his lie. "Everything under the sun, from grizzly and mountain sheep in the Rockies to buffalo and antelope on the prairie. Now I intend to try my hand at something new. Game that will challenge my mettle."

"Challenge your what?"

"Test my ability," Davenport said.

"Gators?" Bodean said.

"Gators," Davenport said, and motioned at Fargo and Morgan and Clementine Purdy and the four other men in new store-bought suits. "We'll be heading into the swamp in the morning and will require the services of a guide. Perhaps you would be so kind as to spread the word?"

"Mister," the beanpole said, "my name is Cleon, and I've lived in this swamp all my life. Take my advice and turn around and go home. It ain't no place for you and yours."

"It's where the gators are," Davenport said.

"And a lot more things, besides," Cleon said. "There's water moccasins and copperheads. There's bogs and quicksand. There's swamp bears, which are meaner than any you'll find in your Rockies, and painters, cats that can pull a man from his horse and drag him off—"

"You exaggerate, surely," Davenport said.

"—and there's the Injuns," Cleon went on as if he hadn't heard. "Some are peaceable but a lot more ain't. You could end up in their cookin' pot if'n you ain't careful."

"Are you suggesting some of them are cannibals?" Davenport said.

"Used to be a lot that were, back in the old days. Now it's just the one tribe but that one tribe is enough." Cleon lowered his voice almost to a whisper. "Ain't you heard of the Kilatku?"

The Kilatku was just one of scores of little-known tribes that lived in the uncharted watery fastness along the Texas and Louisiana coasts. Where a lot of the other tribes had at least some dealings with whites, the Kilatku had none whatsoever. Every white man who dared enter their territory never came out again. It was part of the reason Fargo and the others were there, and about to risk their lives in what he considered a damn silly enterprise.

"You talk too much," Bodean snapped at Cleon.

"They've got a female, consarn you," Cleon said. "They need to know."

"We look after our own, not outsiders," Bodean growled. He unfurled and headed up the street. "We've talked to them enough. Let's go." He pointed at the man with the caterpillar eyebrows. "You, too, Judson."

"Charming fellow," Davenport said.

"A viper is more like it," Fargo said.

Clementine Purdy adjusted her bonnet. "Really, Mr. Fargo. I've only known you a short while but you strike me as terribly cynical. The gentleman called Cleon warned us about the Kilatku, didn't he?"

"You already knew about them."

"We were all thoroughly briefed," Clementine said. "We know what we are letting ourselves in for."

"No, you don't."

"I beg your pardon?"

"You have no damn idea what you're in for, but you're going into the swamp anyway."

"So are you and Major Davenport and Sergeant Morgan and these other soldiers," Clementine said.

"We're men," Fargo said.

"Ah." Clementine scowled. "And you consider me a frail female—is that it?" She sniffed and said, "We all have our duty to perform, I'll have you know."

"Just so it doesn't get us killed," Fargo said.

# Cameron Judd

## *Colter's Path*

When Jedediah "Jedd" Colter hears of a band of travelers bound for the gold fields of California, he uses his hunting skills to convince the Sadler brothers to hire him as a guard. While the journey is difficult and its leaders incompetent, Jedd's natural skills enable him to keep the peace and save them all from disaster.

But when he's injured along the way and the Sadlers head west without him, Jedd has only one thing on his mind—making it to California on his own and getting even with those that did him wrong…

**"Judd is a fine action writer."**
**—*Publishers Weekly***

# Frank Leslie

### DEAD MAN'S TRAIL
When Yakima Henry is attacked by desperados, a mysterious gunman sends the thieves running. But when Yakima goes to thank his savior, he's found dead—with a large poke of gold amongst his gear.

### THE BELLS OF EL DIABLO
A pair of Confederate soldiers go AWOL and head for Denver, where a tale of treasure in Mexico takes them on an adventure.

### THE LAST RIDE OF JED STRANGE
Colter Farrow is forced to kill a soldier in self-defense, sending him to Mexico where he helps the wild Bethel Strange find her missing father. But there's an outlaw on their trail, and the next ones to go missing just might be them...

### DEAD RIVER KILLER
Bad luck has driven Yakima Henry into the town of Dead River during a severe mountain winter—where Yakima must weather a killer who's hell-bent on making the town as dead as its name.

### REVENGE AT HATCHET CREEK
Yakima Henry has been ambushed and badly injured. Luckily, Aubrey Coffin drags him to safety—but as he heals, lawless desperados circle closer to finish the job...

### BULLET FOR A HALF-BREED
Yakima Henry won't tolerate incivility toward a lady, especially the former widow Beth Holgate. If her new husband won't stop giving her hell, Yakima may make her a widow all over again.

**Available wherever books are sold or at
penguin.com**

GRITTY WESTERN ACTION FROM

## *USA TODAY* BESTSELLING AUTHOR
# RALPH COTTON

*SHOWDOWN AT HOLE-IN-THE-WALL*

*RIDERS FROM LONG PINES*

*CROSSING FIRE RIVER*

*ESCAPE FROM FIRE RIVER*

*GUN COUNTRY*

*FIGHTING MEN*

*HANGING IN WILD WIND*

*BLACK VALLEY RIDERS*

*JUSTICE*

*CITY OF BAD MEN*

*GUN LAW*

*SUMMERS' HORSES*

*JACKPOT RIDGE*

*LAWMAN FROM NOGALES*

*SABRE'S EDGE*

*INCIDENT AT GUNN POINT*

*MIDNIGHT RIDER*

*WILDFIRE*

*LOOKOUT HILL*

*VALLEY OF THE GUN*

*BETWEEN HELL AND TEXAS*

*HIGH WILD DESERT*
(COMING APRIL 2013)

Available wherever books are sold or at
penguin.com